CW01622326

Clean Regency Romance

The Duke's Christmas Vow

Arietta Richmond

Dreamstone Publishing © 2020

www.dreamstonepublishing.com

Copyright © 2020 Dreamstone Publishing and Arietta Richmond,

All rights reserved.

No parts of this work may be copied without the author's permission.

ISBN-13: 978-1-925915-77-8

Disclaimer

This is a work of fiction. Names, characters, places, organisations, events, and incidents are either products of the author's imagination or used fictitiously.

Dedication

For everyone who had the grace to be patient while this book, and every other book that I have written, was coming into existence, who provided cups of tea, and food, when the writing would not let me go, and endured countless times being asked for opinions.

For the readers who inspire me to continue writing, by buying my books! Especially for those of you who have taken the time to email me, or to leave reviews, and tell me what you love about my books, and what you'd like to see more of – thank you – I'm listening. I hope that you enjoy book, just as much as my other books.

For my growing team of beta readers and advance reviewers – it's thanks to you that others can enjoy these books in the best presentation possible!

And for all the writers of Regency Historical Romance, whose books I read, who inspired me to write in this fascinating period.

Table of Contents

Books by Arietta Richmond

His Majesty's Hounds

Claiming the Heart of a Duke
Giving a Heart of Lace
Enchanting the Duke
Finding the Duke's Heir
Healing Lord Barton
Loving the Bitter Baron
Rescuing the Countess
Attracting the Spymaster
Intriguing the Viscount
Being Lady Harriet's Hero
Redeeming the Marquess
Winning the Merchant Earl
Kissing the Duke of Hearts
Falling for the Earl
Betting on a Lady's Heart
Courting a Spinster for Christmas
Restoring the Earl's Honour
From Soldier Spy to Lord (contains the first three books in one volume)
To Love a Determined Lady (Contains Books 4, 5 and 6 in one volume)
Love Heals a Lord (Contains Books 7, 8 and 9 in one volume)
To Love a Dashing Lord (Contains Books 10, 11, 12, and 13 in one volume)

A Duke's Daughters – The Elbury Bouquet

A Spinster for a Spy (Lily)
A Vixen for a Viscount (Hyacinth)
A Bluestocking for a Baron (Rose)
A Diamond for a Duke (Camellia)
A Minx for a Merchant (Primrose)
An Enchantress for an Earl (Violet) (coming soon)
A Maiden for a Marquess (Iris) (coming soon)
A Heart for an Heir (Thorne) (coming soon)

The Nettlefold Chronicles

The Duke and the Spinster
A Duke in Autumn
To Dance with the Dangerous Duke
A Christmas Bride for the Duke

The Regency Gothic Series

Lord of the Storm
Lord of the Darkness (coming soon)
Lord of the Lost (coming soon)
Lord of the Shadows (coming soon)

Lady Canterford's Conspirators (The Mayfair Ladies Poetry Society)

A six book series (coming soon)

The Regency Scandals Series

The Gift of a Christmas Scandal
Lady Mariel's Scandalous Love
Christmas with *That* Duke

The Derbyshire Set

A Gift of Love (Prequel short story)
A Devil's Bargain (Prequel short story - coming soon)
The Earl's Unexpected Bride
The Captain's Compromised Heiress
The Viscount's Unsuitable Affair
The Count's Impetuous Seduction
The Rake's Unlikely Redemption
The Marquess' Scandalous Mistress
A Remembered Face (Bonus short story – coming soon)
The Marchioness' Second Chance
A Viscount's Reluctant Passion
Lady Theodora's Christmas Wish
The Duke's Improper Love (coming soon)
A Gentleman's Unconventional Courtship (coming soon)
The Derbyshire Set, Omnibus Edition, Volume 1 (the first three books in one volume.)
The Derbyshire Set, Omnibus Edition, Volume 2 (the second three books in one volume.)

Other Books

The Scottish Governess
Her Summer Duke
Her Passionate Duke
Her Absent Duke
Her Determined Duke
Her Generous Duke (Coming Soon)
The Duke's Christmas Vow
Her Christmas Duke (Coming Soon)
The Crew of the Seadragon's Soul Series, (coming soon - a set of 10 linked novels)

Themed Collections

The Regency Christmas Hearts Collection
The Regency Spring and Valentine's Hearts Collection
The Regency Summer Hearts Collection
The Regency Autumn Hearts Collection

Prologue

Christmas Day 1816

"Your solemn vow, Rafael. Give me your solemn vow that you will find a suitable woman to marry, before next Christmas Day."

Rafael Livingstone, Duke of Oakmoor, regarded his mother with an expression compounded of frustration, resentment, and resignation. They were barely a week out of their year of mourning for his father and, already, it had come to this. He knew that he should marry, and get himself an heir, that it was part of the responsibility which came with the title, but he had hoped for a few years respite from the London Season, and the hovering hopeful young women who wished to be a Duchess.

Mourning had allowed him to avoid their shallow falsity for a year, but now, it seemed that there was to be no further escape.

“Surely, I can take a little more time about it? I would prefer to find a woman I might actually like, or even love, rather than simply tolerate! And I’ve yet to meet one. Every young woman of the *ton* that I have met is vapid, insipid, shallow, self-serving, and prone to gossip and lies. I abhor gossip, and dishonesty is just completely unacceptable.”

“Nonetheless, I want your solemn vow. There must be one woman among them that you can tolerate. You cannot waste time – you need an heir. The thought that, if anything should happen to you, the title and estates would go to your uncle, is enough to make any sane person feel quite ill. Your uncle is incapable, bedridden – the estates would fall into disrepair, and everything that your father and his father worked for would be lost.”

Rafe, nodded, unable to dispute her point. What she said was true. He swallowed, facing the fact that he would have to give her what she wanted, that duty bound him despite his personal misgivings. He would give his vow, and pray that a miracle happened, that somehow, he would meet a suitable woman, who was also pleasant, honest, straightforward, and had at least a modicum of intelligence.

“All right Mother. I give you my vow. By next Christmas Day, I will find a woman to marry.”

“Thank you. But I warn you, don’t take this lightly. If, by November, you have not become betrothed, I will organise a Christmas House Party, and you will choose from amongst those who attend.”

Rafe shuddered.

“I will do my best to prevent it coming to that.”

Chapter One

December 1817

Lady Charity Pemberton breathed deeply of the crisp wintry air. There was a touch of the scent of the sea to it, for Oakmoor Chase was close to the coast, a vast estate of forest and moor, which ran from rolling hills to dramatic sea cliffs. It was beautiful, in a stark kind of way. Above her, sea birds wheeled through the clouded sky, crying their mournful cries.

She felt a kinship with them, as if they cried for what they would never have, as she had often done. She shook her head. She should not be maudlin – the day was beautiful, she had already found a number of wonderful feathers, and it was nearing Christmas. The fact that she was at a Christmas House Party, where she knew no one else, and at which her mother desperately hoped she would attract the attention of the Duke strongly enough to get him to court her, should not be allowed to spoil her pleasure in the day.

Determination filled her. She would do her best. She needed to marry well, if she possibly could, for her family was, although titled, rather poor.

Still, the thought of conversing with the Duke sent chills through her. She was hopeless at acceptable social conversation – she was far too honest, too blunt, too prone to answering questions before considering what would be the most polite thing to say. And, whilst she was by no means ugly, she was not beautiful – she was, instead, ordinary, and only stood out in company because of her dreadful dark red hair.

She pushed those thoughts aside with a sigh – there was nothing she could do to change any of it.

Both sides of the lane she was walking down were lined by high hedges of holly bushes, blocking the view of the fields beyond. The ground beneath her feet was crusted with frost, which crunched at every step, but there had been no snow for days. Ahead of her, she could see that the lane turned, but she could see no further than that bend. She would, she supposed, discover what was there, as soon as she reached that spot – but right now, she stopped – for, caught in the prickly leaves of the bushes, high up, was a magnificent, brilliantly white feather – from a gull, she suspected.

She carefully set down her small covered basket, and stepped as close to the hedge as she could, without suffering too many pricklings from the leaves, and reached up for the feather. She was too short. Her fingertips were still inches below it. She tried jumping, but her pelisse snagged on the leaves, and she nearly fell. Carefully untangling herself, she tried again.

She still failed to capture the feather, but this time, as she dropped back towards the ground, she collided with something, hard.

*****

Rafe had risen before dawn, and slipped out of the house to walk across the fields, and along the cliffs. The crisp air shocked him fully awake, and sight of the dawn above the sea was familiar and reassuring, reminding him that beauty still existed, naturally. A reminder he needed when he currently had a house full of young ladies whose beauty was so artificial as to seem almost theatrical.

Now, he was striding down the lane, going back towards the house. If he was not visible in the breakfast room soon, his mother would nag at him again. It was his own fault, he supposed – he had vowed to her that he would find a woman to marry by this Christmas, but the year had gone by alarmingly fast, and here he was, still not betrothed, and therefore holding this damned house party.

Just the thought of it ruffled the calm he had achieved. He walked faster, almost charging around the bend in the lane – and ran straight into something – someone... instinctively, his arms went out, to catch whoever it was.

And that made it instantly apparent that it was a woman. Her back was to him, and his arms had ended up around her waist. The front of the skirts of her pelisse seemed to be entangled in the hedge, and her rather plain bonnet was askew on her head. That fact revealed a mass of curling dark red hair which was quite magnificent. Which also tickled his nose.

He moved, carefully adjusting his grip on her, and reached out with one hand to untangle her skirts from the hedge. Thus released, she turned in his arms, which meant that she was almost pressed against him, face to face.

Deep violet toned eyes met his. For a moment, he forgot to breathe. There was nothing artificial about the face before him. No cosmetics enhanced it – it was perfect, just as it was.

Her lips, as naturally dark red as that hair, parted in surprise, and she blushed. He should release her – such an intimate hold on an unchaperoned young woman he did not know was well and truly beyond the bounds of propriety.

But he did not. Instead, he had the shocking urge to kiss those lips which were so very close to his.

"I… I'm sorry… I was… I fell…"

Her voice was as natural and beautiful as the rest of her. But it jolted him out of his daze, and he rapidly released her, first making sure that she was stable on her feet. He stepped back a pace, putting a safe distance between them. A tiny frown crossed her brow, as if she had not wished him to move – but that was a silly conceit – no woman would want to be unceremoniously manhandled in a country lane.

"There's no need to apologise. I was thinking, walking too fast, and not looking where I was going. I am sure that you would have been quite all right if I had not collided with you."

She blushed again, and turned her eyes away from him for a moment.

"If I had not been distracted, I might have seen you coming, rather than being in a position to be collided with."

He looked at her – distracted? What did she mean? What had she been doing? There was nothing here but the frosted ground of the lane, and the high hedges bordering it.

"Distracted? What were you doing, that distracted you, and got your skirts caught in the hedge?"

She blushed again, a deep red, seeming intensely embarrassed, then lifted a hand to point upwards. At first, he had no idea what she was pointing at – then he realised that there was something white, stuck amongst the leaves, quite high up.

"I... I was trying to reach the feather. Sadly, I am too short to do so – and being holly, it's not the sort of hedge I can scramble into..."

Rafe felt his eyebrow rise – why would she want a feather? But he did not ask – it was none of his business, and if the Lady wanted a feather, there was no reason she shouldn't have it. He reached up, carefully extracted it from the prickly leaves, and presented it to her with a bow.

She took it with a curtsey.

"Thank you. I... I'll be on my way now. I am sorry for disrupting your walk."

She scooped up a small covered basket, which he had not noticed until that moment, slipped the feather into it, and set off down the lane. He stood and watched her go, bemused, and more than a little intrigued. She rounded the bend and disappeared from his view.

He had no idea who she was. And suddenly, that felt like a bad thing.

He shook his head, and set off again, walking as fast as he could, but now paying far more attention to his surroundings.

*****

Charity stopped as soon as she had gone a little way past the bend in the lane.

She was shaking.

That had been... she was almost certain that had been... the Duke. The man whose house party she was attending, with her mother. The man her mother hoped would find her so attractive that he would want to marry her.

And he had discovered her leaping about in a country lane like a small child, chasing a feather. She was mortified.

It was bad enough that she was plain, that they couldn't afford a better quality of gowns for her, that she was awkward in social situations, but now, she'd made the kind of first impression on a man which almost certainly guaranteed that he would find her laughable. No one understood why she collected feathers – in fact, almost no one knew that she did. Nor did they know what she did with them.

For what she did was perilously unrespectable, for it amounted to partaking in trade. The fact that the money she made from it was necessary to their survival at times did not make it any better. In the eyes of the *ton*, if it became known, she would be a pariah.

Once the shakes settled, she walked on, taking her time before returning to the house, lest she come across him again. At least he had not mocked her for her childishness in seeking a feather, or her foolishness in getting herself caught on the hedge. And he was, of a certainty, the most handsome man she had ever seen. His attire had been of the best, yet simple, of plain colours and sturdy construction. And that moment when his eyes had met hers, as she stood in the circle of his arms - just the memory of it made her blush again.

He had looked at her as if he found her desirable. Which was quite the most wonderful thing which had ever happened to her.

She laughed at the thought. It had been disastrous, and wonderful, all at the same time. But she had best make sure that she was perfectly presented this afternoon, that she pretended their meeting had never occurred, and that she prayed he did not tell others of it, as an anecdote to laugh about.

That thought made her shiver with fear.

Her family depended on her – she had to marry well, and soon, or, after two years of poor crops, their crippling debts would become impossible.

Her father was far older than her mother, and an invalid – if she did not marry before he died, she was not at all sure what would become of them.

Yet... most men frightened her, in one way or another. Some were overbearing, arrogant and domineering, others were foppish, strange in their habits, and quite disturbingly odd. She needed to find a man who was not only someone she could countenance spending time with, but one who would not mind the near vanishing smallness of her dowry, and one who might help support her mother, when her father's inevitable death arrived and his title, as well as all but a few properties, went to her uncle.

She turned, and made her way back in the direction of the house, finding another three feathers along the way, and determinedly set her mind to forgetting all about being held in the Duke's arms.

*****

The breakfast room was full. He felt as if his mother had invited every unmarried woman in the *ton* to this House Party.

They fluttered about, all watching for any chance to place themselves in his path. Their mothers and fathers watched them, hopeful. The other men who attended – mainly brothers of the women, and a few who were actually his friends – watched the women, attempting, he suspected, to ascertain which ones Rafe wasn't interested in, so that they might consider them for themselves.

It made eating a peaceful breakfast an impossibility. There was no way to eat even something so simple as toast and marmalade, and still carry on vaguely polite conversation. So he said as little as possible – let them think him rude – and escaped to his study as soon as he could, despite the glare his mother gave him as he left the breakfast room.

Chapter Two

Charity slipped back into the house, and up to her rooms, asking a maid she passed on the way to have a breakfast tray sent up for her. She simply could not face the idea of a breakfast room full of people, not after her embarrassing morning encounter. All of the other young ladies she had seen here were beautiful, polished, perfectly presented, and seemingly accomplished – everything she was not. Especially now, with pulled threads on her pelisse skirts, and her bonnet askew.

She would hide away for the morning, perhaps work on the bonnet decoration she was making, and only go down in the afternoon, when she had changed, and made herself as presentable as possible. In her rooms, she set the basket down on the small escritoire set near the window of the little parlour, and went into her dressing room. Maggie was there, carefully pressing each of Charity's gowns, mending small imperfections, and hanging them on the hooks along the wall, so that they might be ready when Charity needed them. They had only arrived here the previous night, so Maggie still had a lot of unpacking to do.

"Maggie, I'd like to change please. I think that I managed to prevent my hems becoming mud stained, but... I'm terribly sorry, I've managed to snag threads on this pelisse, which will need to be mended."

The maid looked up, her expression momentarily fearful, until her eyes came to rest on the front of Charity's garments – then her face cleared.

"There's no need to apologise, my Lady – I can fix pulled threads like that easily. Which gown would you like to change into?"

Charity felt a surge of relief – Maggie had enough to do, caring for both Charity and her mother, without her life being made harder by Charity's carelessness.

"The blue one, I think. And... can you please fix my hair? I... I got it caught on a hedge."

Maggie smiled at her, half laughing.

"Did you get the feather you were trying to reach, my Lady? For that's the only reason I can think of for you to get tangled in a hedge."

Charity nodded, returning the girl's smile, and submitted to Maggie's efficient attentions to her attire.

Twenty minutes later, wearing the blue gown, and with her hair pinned neatly back into a pile of coils on her head, Charity sat at the escritoire, and carefully unpacked her gatherings from the morning's walk.

The white feather was, truly, magnificent.

It was large, and none of the fine threads which comprised it had been misaligned. It was absolutely perfect to be the final part of the bonnet decoration she had been making.

But the image which came to her mind as she touched it was not that decoration, but instead, the deep brown eyes of the man who had gathered it for her. She stared out of the window at the fields below, where they ran in a long rolling moor towards the sea, and despite her intention to forget about the sensation of being held in a man's arms, she relived that moment, over and over, in her thoughts.

And came to a startling realisation.

She hadn't, not for one moment, felt frightened by him. Nor had she found him disturbing in any way – well, except for the way that his hands around her had made her heart beat faster. And that was not a bad kind of disturbing...

Apart from her father, she could not remember any other man who had not made her feel either frightened or disturbed. A half choked-off sob escaped her. Of course, the first man she discovered who she found even vaguely interesting, and non-threatening, had to be a Duke – a Duke surrounded by other young women, all far more suitable to be his bride than Charity ever could be.

*****

It was mid-afternoon, and Rafe knew that he could avoid it no longer – he would have to go down to the parlour, and take tea with his guests. Which meant engaging in conversation with all of the young women present. If he tried to isolate himself with the few of his men friends who were here, his mother was just as like to simply march into their conversation, and remove him from it by some thin excuse. He sighed, and called for his valet – if he must do it, he had best look as presentable as possible.

Half an hour later, as well presented as if he was about to attend a London soiree, he went downstairs. He could hear the murmur of conversation before he was half way down – a susurrus of female voices. He paused just outside the parlour door, taking a steadying breath, and considered, just for moment, turning, and leaving the house. He did not do it, of course, for he had given his mother his vow, and somehow, he would stay true to it.

He opened the door and went in. The conversation immediately hushed, and all eyes turned in his direction. He felt, in that instant, like a stallion in the ring at Tattersall's, being eyed by potential buyers. It was not a pleasant sensation. His mother came to him, her expression making it clear, subtly, that she thought he should have made his appearance rather sooner.

"Oakmoor – do come and let me introduce you to some of our guests whom you have not yet become acquainted with."

"Of course, Mother."

The Duchess led him across the room, and Rafe carefully studied the people present, all without actually looking too directly at anyone. Various young ladies watched him, some with considerably more hope in their expressions than others. He had met most of them yesterday, but a few had arrived very late, and had not been down to the breakfast room before he had retreated to his rooms.

There were, he had to admit, some quite stunningly beautiful young women here – but still, they all seemed rather artificial – too studied, as if they had no life outside of being decorative.

Unbidden, the face of the young woman he had collided with on the lane came back to him – a face beautiful because it was genuine and unaffected.

It had been, he realised now, a quite remarkable meeting, for she had made no attempt to simper at him, had not taken advantage, at all, of being in his arms for those few moments. He doubted that almost any woman in this room would have been so reticent.

They reached a cluster of people who stood near the large bay window which overlooked the gardens, and his mother came to a stop.

"Ladies... if I may interrupt your conversation to perform introductions..."

They turned at her voice, their conversation dying away. There were seven women – three older, and likely the mothers of the younger ones, and four younger, two of whom looked so alike that there was no doubt of their kinship.

One of the older women spoke, addressing his mother, but eyeing him curiously.

"Of course, Your Grace."

"Ladies, I would like to make known to you my son, the Duke of Oakmoor, your host for this party. Oakmoor, I present to you the Countess of Chilwinth and her daughter, Lady Anne Brooks; the Baroness Delfanning and her daughters Miss Woodfield and Miss Penelope Woodfield; and the Marchioness of Warkworth, and her daughter Lady Charity Pemberton."

There were curtsies, and many murmurs of greeting, but Rafe was barely aware of any of it. He was, instead, frozen in place, his eyes locked on those of the last lady introduced - wide violet toned eyes which he had last looked into that very morning, in a frosty country lane, from far closer than was proper. That wealth of deep red curls had been tamed, and pinned into artful coils on her head, but no other artifice had been applied to her.

Which was more than he could say for the other three young women. So, now he knew her name – which only made her the more intriguing, for he would have expected a Marquess' daughter to be like all of the others. Instead, her gown was quite plain, if of excellent quality, the colour in her lips and cheeks was natural, and her expression held more of fear and trepidation than of simpering obsequiousness.

What was she afraid of? Rafe had never thought himself particularly fierce in mien and that morning, in the lane, whilst she had seemed embarrassed, he had seen no sign of fear. Silence fell, lengthened and, seemingly at the same moment, Rafe and the girl before him recognised that fact. He tore his eyes away from hers, even as her face assumed a bland and polite smile.

"I am delighted to meet all of you, ladies. I hope that you will enjoy your stay at Oakmoor Chase this Christmas Season."

The artificial ones all seemed to speak at once, assuring him in an effusive manner that they would. But the response which struck him most strongly came from Lady Charity – a response spoken so softly that he would not have heard it had not she been the closest to him at the time.

"I hope so too..."

He caught her eyes again, and she flushed, looking away, as if embarrassed that he had heard. As his mother led him away from them to the other set of late arrivals to whom he had not yet been introduced, his mind stayed with Lady Charity. He had the strangest feeling that she had spoken honestly with those words, had simply answered him, without stopping to consider exactly what to say or do. Intriguing... absolutely intriguing – for it implied that she had spoken honestly, rather than concocting a response which she thought was what he would want to hear. The novelty of such a response was immense.

He was soon introduced to another two young ladies and their parents, before his mother released him to circulate amongst the guests himself. Obedient to what he had promised her, he made certain to speak to each of the eligible young women in the room – but he also made certain that he spent no more time with any one than any other. He would not give them grounds for hope of his interest.

He found himself, without having intended to, tracking where in the room Lady Charity was. She had barely moved from near the bay window, and did not appear to be involved in any of the conversations around her. He almost laughed as he realised that, in that moment, he envied her – if he had been able to avoid conversation, he would have done so.

Perhaps later, he might find a chance to speak with her, to discover if she was truly as different as she seemed – and, if he could, to discover what that expression of apparent fear had been about.

*****

When the Duchess had performed the introductions, Charity had wished, for a moment, that the floor might open up and swallow her. Fear had filled her – fear that he might remark on their early morning meeting, revealing that she had been out unchaperoned, or that he might treat her with disdain.

When neither thing happened, and she had instead found her gaze locked to his, she had been hard pressed to look away, even as the silence extended. She did not understand what she saw in his expression – he studied her, as if she was a puzzle that he needed to unravel. She only hoped that the other young women present had not noticed that moment between them.

He had looked away at the same moment she had, and made polite conversation, ending with that hope that they would enjoy their stay at Oakmoor Chase. She had responded automatically, without pausing to think first, and then horrified embarrassment had filled her when she had realised what she had done, and that he had actually heard her! He had met her eyes again, and she had braced herself for an expression of scorn, but instead had seen only curiosity in that gaze, before she had looked down.

Now, as he moved around the room, talking to everyone, but to no one for very long, she could not help but watch him. Blessedly, the other women near her became caught up in various conversations, including her mother, and Charity was able to simply sit on the bay window seat and sip at her tea, without needing to deal with the exhausting process of polite conversation. Exhausting because it required her to weigh every word before she spoke, lest she blurt out something blunt and inappropriate.

Not far from her, Lady Anne Brooks and the Misses Woodfield were talking to each other quietly, their voices coming clearly to Charity where she sat.

"Have you heard what is being said about this house party, Miss Woodfield?"

Lady Anne's voice was lowered in that manner which people used when discussing things secret or scandalous.

"What is being said, Lady Anne?"

Miss Woodfield leant close to Lady Anne, her eyes alight, and her sister pressed closer too.

"It is rumoured that the Duke has made a vow to choose a woman to be his bride – from those present at this very party!"

"Oh! Then... perhaps there is some pattern to who has been invited? For we seem an interesting mix of people – some from the first stare of fashionable society, and some who are far less commonly seen about in London. Do you think... do you think that the Duke has already considered others, and come to a narrowed range of choices? That perhaps we are here because we are strong contenders to be his Duchess?"

"That is an exciting thought, Miss Woodfield, is it not?"

"It is. Although... given the... variety... of those present, if that is the case, then the Duke has remarkably... eclectic taste in women!"

"You are correct there. I must say, there are some people here whom I would not have expected... but perhaps they are here so that his gentlemen friends will have young ladies to consider as well?"

"Possibly..."

They moved off at that point, going to stand near the fire, and Charity was left alone to consider what she had heard. Above her, across the top of the bay window, a string of tiny Christmas bells hung, twined with ribbon and sprigs of holly. Every so often, the movement of the air in the room caused them to ring softly, as they did at that moment.

Charity looked up, and smiled when she saw the holly – it reminded her of that morning, of the huge hedges of it, and the feather... and the Duke.

The Duke, who might be specifically intending to choose a bride in the next week, from amongst the women here. If she had thought her mother's hope was improbable before, now Charity knew it to be so unlikely as to be laughable. The chance of Charity attracting the Duke's courtship was vanishingly small.

She studied all of the young women present, sipping her tea, and pretending to be completely at ease.

They were uniformly beautiful – more so than she – and their appearance was polished to perfection. They wore gowns from the best modistes, jewels from the most skilled goldsmiths, and delicate bejewelled slippers. They conversed with perfect ease, about the inconsequential nothings which comprised polite discussion, and moved elegantly. No doubt they also played the pianoforte to perfection, painted exquisite watercolours of boring subjects, and embroidered such fine stitches that one would need a quizzing glass to see them properly.

Charity was not even one of those things – except perhaps for the quality of her sewing – but her stitches were done on prosaic things like repairing her gowns, or stitching the feathers onto a headdress, not on pointless but pretty handkerchiefs and the like. She sipped her tea again, and watched as the Duke moved to yet another cluster of young ladies, always smiling, and obviously at ease joining them in speaking of polite nothings.

No matter what her mother hoped for, Charity had best resign herself to invisibility, and be thankful for it. There was not the slightest possibility of the Duke being interested in her, especially not after the manner of their first meeting.

Chapter Three

"Well Rafael, what do you think of them? These are the last of the young ladies of the *ton* who might be remotely suitable. After you decided against so many during the Season, and then again in Bath in autumn, I despaired of finding enough respectable young women to invite for this house party. Now you must fulfil your vow, and chose one of them."

Rafe regarded his mother with a rueful smile.

"I know that I gave my word... but..."

"I warned you not to take that vow lightly. If none of them strike you strongly, you must simply choose the one who annoys you least, and have done with it."

Rafe winced at her words, trying to imagine living with the young women he had been speaking to that day. Although he had been as even handed as he possibly could with how much time he spent with each, they had all been attempting to manipulate things to get more time with him.

Not all.

The thought slipped into his mind, unbidden. There was one young woman who had made no attempt to get close to him. One young woman whose face bore no artifice, and whose deep violet eyes were imprinted on his memory.

He shook his head – perhaps she was simply trying a different tactic, attempting to interest him by not forcing herself upon him. If that was the tactic, then she was at least partially succeeding, he thought, a little chagrined. But it was only the third day of this house party – there was still a week and a half to go before Christmas, before he would be forced to choose. Surely, in that time, he could determine enough of the character of each of the ladies who were present, to be able to choose?

"I gave my word, so I will choose one. But not until the very last day, unless I do truly become taken with one of them. Between now and then, I will continue to spend equal time with each one, if I can, and to avoid, very vigorously, any attempt on their part to trap me in a compromise – for I am sure that some of them will try that tactic."

"Thank you. And yes, they likely will. As far as I can tell, the rumour has already circulated amongst them, that you plan to choose a bride here. I would suggest that you are cautious around Lady Anne Brooks – she strikes me as rather determined and forward, and I know that her family are not as wealthy as they like to imply."

"Thank you for the warning, Mother. I have no particular concern for the wealth of my bride's family, or the size of her dowry – we do not lack for wealth – but equally, I will not be manipulated into having to rescue her family from the depredations of a wastrel father, grandfather, or brother. If I help her family, should it be necessary, then it will be by my choice."

"Very wise of you, Rafael. Truthfully, I would not have invited her, had we not been so short on remaining possibilities for ladies you had not already rejected as unsuitable."

"Well then, you can cross her off the list of candidates now – I assume that you do have a list, Mother?"

His mother laughed softly.

"Of course I do – you know that I am always organised, if nothing else."

"Indeed."

"I will leave you to contemplate your options. But don't attempt to hide away here in your study for too long."

"I won't. But I will stay here for a little while, and do as you suggest – contemplate them all. I rather think that quite a few will be crossed off that list quickly."

His mother sighed at those words, but nodded, and left the room. Rafe sat, staring at the family portrait which hung on the study wall – it showed his parents, with him and his sister Mercy, when they had been children – before Rafe had gone off to Eton. His mother was right – he did not wish to allow his father's legacy to be lost. He needed a wife, and an heir. He had hoped for the sort of happiness which Mercy had found, for she had married for love, some seven years earlier, but it seemed that he was not to have that, so he had best resign himself to his fate.

He mentally ran through the list of young ladies present – there were ten, each with one or both parents attending with them. Most were very much typical of the *ton*, with middling figures, dressed in pale colours, with hair of various shades from mid-brown to pale blonde, and pale skin, enhanced with careful cosmetics to cover freckles and the like, and make them seem flushed with health.

They were like so many children – each vying for his attention, each wanting the prize, each thinking only of herself.

Not all.

The thought came again.

Lady Charity Pemberton seemed different – her skin was flushed with genuine health, with no artifice needed, her hair was a rich dark red, and her garments, whilst rather plain, were well made, and seemed to feature slightly stronger colours – enough that he noticed her, in any room. And she did not simper at him, did not push herself forward – had, in fact, been barely visible.

He had only noted where she was because, since their meeting in the lane, he had found himself looking for her.

Could she be a suitable option?

He did not know. He knew nothing of her family, beyond the fact that the Warkworth March was an old title, and he had not ever heard gossip about it… wait, he had, but just once – something about Lady Charity's father being far older than her mother, and society having been a little scandalised by their marriage at the time. Nothing beyond that – and a scandal more than twenty years gone was irrelevant to today.

Perhaps he should seek her out, and speak to her more – but he would need to be careful, lest the other young women see it as him preferring her. He would not be at all surprised if some of them were capable of quite malicious actions towards one they saw as competition – and he would not wish to bring that upon Lady Charity.

She deserved better.

That thought surprised him, yet he felt it to be true.

He rose, and left the room – he was no further ahead in his deliberations, beyond that intent to seek out Lady Charity, and it was best that he steel himself, and go back to interacting with them. He would never reach a decision if he simply avoided all of them until Christmas Day.

*****

Charity had spent the morning in her rooms, carefully constructing a rather flamboyant feathered piece for her mother's evening wear. Her mother liked wearing the turban like headdresses, for the simple reason that they could be economically repurposed, over and over again, by changing the feathers attached, and adding or removing some layers of cloth.

The previous day had been cold, with a drizzle of rain in the morning, and she had not ventured out. All day, she had made sure that she was inconspicuous – listening to the other young women discuss the Duke, and finding herself rather offended on his behalf by their attitudes. Which was ridiculous – he was, in no way, hers to defend.

Tomorrow, she would go for a walk in the early morning again – so that she need not take a chaperone, and could search for feathers as she liked with no one the wiser. It was rather improper of her to go out alone, but she would do so, nonetheless, else she would go quite mad. Her mother had looked at her just this morning, and shaken her head sighing, then asked her quietly if she could at least try to capture the Duke's attention.

Charity had said that she would, but in all honesty, she could not imagine how she might manage it.

Now, as afternoon approached, she set the finished piece carefully on the dresser, beside her mother's turban, and called Maggie to help her change. It was time to go downstairs, and mingle with the other guests.

The parlour was full, with some of the older people playing cards at a table set to one side, and the other young women clustered in two groups. One group were gathered near the fireplace, and the other in the corner, not far from the bay window. Charity paused a moment just inside the door. Her mother was at the card table, and obviously deeply engaged in the conversation there, as well as the game. Which meant that going to her was not an option.

Charity considered the room again. The bay window seat seemed her best choice. She had a small journal in her pockets, and a pencil – she could sit in the bay window seat, being thereby partially hidden from the others by the curtains, and sketch designs for feathered brooches and hats. If anyone saw them, they would simply think her a little eccentric, to sketch such things rather than the view out of the window – they would certainly not suspect that she sketched them with the intent of making them later.

She moved across the room, as usual, barely noticed by anyone, for they were all too busy with their conversations. Upon reaching the bay window, she was tempted to slide back onto the seat, and curl her feet up under her – but with a little inward sigh, she reminded herself that she should not – that to do so would be far too casual and childlike for a proper young lady. So she sat to one side, leaning back against the wall – which meant that she was very much tucked behind the curving bundle of the tied curtains on that side - but she did not care, for being inconspicuous was her preference, anyway.

The Duke, she realised, was not in the room – she looked for him, almost unconsciously, each time she entered a room – so that she could avoid him, she told herself – certainly not because she cared what he did. Still, her mother would be disappointed...

The other side of the curtain which hid her, someone stood talking. Charity realised that she could hear them very clearly – perhaps it was some trick of the shape of the room, and the position of the curtains, but their conversation seemed to be funnelled towards her, along the wall, and past the edge of the curtain. She should ignore them – it was impolite to eavesdrop – but curiosity drove her – and if she moved from here, where else in the room might she go?

At least one of the voices seemed familiar, and after a moment, she realised that it was Lady Anne Brooks. Lady Anne struck Charity as being very sure of her own charms, and very forward – but perhaps that was simply a perception created by the comparison to Charity's own rather reticent nature. The voices continued, and even as Charity sketched a hat, she listened.

"You must try harder, Anne! He spends no more time with you than any of the others – that will not do at all!"

"But Mama, I do try! Unlike other gentlemen, he does not seem to even notice my bosom, nor does he even really look at me when we speak together. Nor has he kissed my hand. How can I garner more of his attention when he behaves like that?"

"Perhaps one of your more daring gowns? And you must discover what he is interested in, and ask him to tell you about it – men like talking about themselves, and you can look adoring and fascinated."

“I have tried Mama – but he has no interest in hunting, nor in telling me about the size of his estates, nor any of the other things that gentlemen will usually talk about!”

“Then… perhaps, if he does not begin to show interest soon, we will have to apply more drastic measures.”

Charity had almost ceased to breathe – she should not be overhearing this, yet she could not move without potentially revealing her position. The conversation sickened her, for it was obvious that the two women spoke of the Duke, and Lady Anne’s attempts to ensnare his affections. The very idea that they sought to manipulate him was horrifying – what kind of marriage would a person have, if it was based, from the start, on deceit and manipulation? And that last remark… what had Lady Chilwinth meant by *‘more drastic measures’*?

After a moment of silence, Lady Anne spoke again.

“Mama… you don’t mean…?”

“I do. If it takes a suitably arranged discovery of you, with him in an unequivocally shocking situation, to bring him up to snuff, then so be it.”

Charity bit her lip in her effort not to gasp. They were talking about trying to intentionally compromise the Duke! She had heard of such things happening, but had never expected to meet a person so unscrupulous as to attempt something so dreadfully improper. Lady Anne was speaking again.

“Mama… how might we achieve that? Will it not be difficult, if he does not attempt to spend any time with me?”

“It will, but I will think of a way – I will watch closely everything that he does, what the routine of his days is like, and discover something that we can take advantage of. There will be something, I am sure.”

"I will watch also, whilst I continue to try to attract him – what kind of man does not respond to flattery?"

One worth knowing.

The thought slipped into Charity's mind. There were very few men she had ever met about whom she would have said that, but the Duke of Oakmoor definitely qualified. Should she warn him? But how could she, without being alone with him? Which was most unlikely to happen. It worried her – she would not wish to see him trapped by the likes of Lady Anne, yet she could see no way that she could act to prevent it. She would simply have to be alert to both what chances she might have to speak to him alone, and to what Lady Anne was doing.

Lady Anne and her mother moved away, and Charity breathed easier – but she could not concentrate on drawing – her mind was too busy, replaying what she had heard, and worrying.

*****

Rafe stepped into the parlour and, as usual, all eyes turned towards him. He forced himself to smile. Now for the difficult bit – he could not go directly to any one group where one or more of the young ladies were engaged in conversation, or that would be interpreted as preference, so he would need to engineer a more casual approach to conversation.

Fortunately, his mother stood near the card table, and, as he moved in her direction, it appeared that the current game concluded, and various people rose, as others took their places. By the time he reached his mother, she was speaking with Lady Warkworth.

Who was joined at that moment by her daughter.

Rafe felt oddly pleased – if he had to speak to these young women, Lady Charity would be his first choice of them all – for she would not, he already knew, blather on at him about inconsequentialities. She looked up, and met his eyes, hers filled with some consternation. He frowned, wondering what disturbed her so.

"Good afternoon Mother, Lady Warkworth, Lady Charity. I trust that you are well today?"

He bowed, and they curtsied in return, all save his mother. As she rose, Lady Charity spoke, her voice quite soft and melodious.

"I am indeed well, Your Grace, thank you."

It was as before – she seemed simply to answer when spoken to, with no thought to flattering him, or simpering, or... anything but the simplicity of truth. It was, in comparison to other women, quite startling. He smiled at her, suddenly pleased, and for a moment, she met his eyes again, with that open regard that he had first seen in the frosty lane. Then, after mere seconds, that clouded over into uncertainty again.

He had to find out why.

Chapter Four

Charity cringed inside. There was nothing pretty or elegant about her speech – she always just blurted out the simplest answer. Yet the Duke had smiled at her... she turned her eyes away. He was just being kind to her, kind to the awkward, plain girl. She was foolish to think that she might ever get to speak to him privately enough to warn him of Lady Anne's scheming, yet she felt that she should try.

He did not deserve to be trapped by the likes of Lady Anne. Yet... she did not know what he wanted, and it was most arrogant of her to make presumptions on the matter. If he was truly seeking to choose a bride, what manner of woman might he want? Did he care for love? Or did he only care for her appearance, and the other practical qualities which the woman might bring to the marriage? Most men of the *ton*, as far as she knew, did not regard love as important. And a Duchess should be polished and socially skilled – so perhaps someone as adept at manipulation as Lady Anne would be a benefit to him?

She shook her head, frustrated.

The Duke was saying something to her mother – something about there being plans for some more formal dinners, and dancing, over the next week. Charity barely prevented herself from shuddering – more chances for her social ineptness to be on display, in a room full of beautifully polished young women. The conversation finished, and the Duke moved on to speak to another group of people. Charity felt as if the warmth in the room moved with him – suddenly, she was cold, and more disconsolate than ever.

She watched him move around the room, and could not help but study the moment when he reached the group where Lady Anne stood with Lady Chilwinth. Lady Anne immediately assumed a bright smile, and blushed becomingly when the Duke bowed to her. She appeared to be chattering away about something – what on earth did she find to talk about?

The Duke, however, rather to Charity's surprise, looked almost bored – perhaps he had no interest in whatever topic she spoke of?

Watching was pointless. Charity made herself turn away – only to discover her mother watching her.

"So, daughter, you find him of interest, do you? That is most unusual for you."

"I... ah... well... he is not so... overbearing... as most men."

Her mother lifted a hand to her chest in mock surprise.

"There is hope yet..."

"Mother! It is not as if he will notice me anyway – not amongst all of these oh-so-polished young ladies."

"Nonetheless..."

"I know. I will try."

At that moment, one of the older ladies approached to speak to her mother, and Charity allowed herself to sink back into silence, simply observing the room. Which was why, an hour or so later, she noticed Lady Anne exit the room not long after the Duke had done so.

Her heart beat harder, and her mouth went dry – was this arranged between Lady Anne and the Duke? Or was her leaving the first step in her attempting to trap him? If it was the latter, then she simply could not let it happen – not without trying to do something!

Charity whispered in her mother's ear that she needed the necessary, and slipped quietly across the room, and into the hallway. To one side, she saw a flash of movement – the tail of Lady Anne's skirts disappearing through a door. Moving as rapidly as she could, she went in that direction.

It seemed that she was just in time, for she reached the door to see, before Lady Anne had a chance to close it, the Duke rising from his seat behind his desk. He spoke, sounding somewhat shocked, even as his eyes found Charity, where she stood in the hall.

"Lady Anne! What are you doing here?"

Charity chose that moment to 'accidentally' bump against a side table, causing it to thump against the wall. Lady Anne looked around, startled, and for a moment her expression was such that, if looks could kill, Charity would have perished on the spot. Then she turned back, assuming a startled and innocent expression, and gasped.

"Oh, Your Grace, I do apologise… I was looking for the necessary, and I must have taken a wrong turn!"

The deceitful girl even managed to flush with apparent embarrassment at having to mention something so improper to a man. Charity spoke up.

"Lady Anne, it just so happens that I am on my way to the necessary too – let me guide you."

The Duke gave Charity a very grateful smile, and bowed.

"There, Lady Anne, a solution to your problem. Do not let me delay you."

Lady Anne, left with no options, turned with the appearance of good grace, and stepped out into the hallway. The Duke closed the door behind her, and Charity heard the click as it locked. How very wise of him.

"It's this way, Lady Anne."

The woman glared at Charity, and it was very obvious that retribution was likely, later – Charity would need to take great care. But what could she have done? She could not simply have allowed the unscrupulous woman to trap the Duke!

"I did not need your assistance, Lady Charity."

The words were hissed, and the venom in them shocked Charity – and drove her uncharacteristically, to respond sharply.

"Oh dear, Lady Anne, are you sure, it looked remarkably like you were lost – or at least that is what I heard you tell the Duke. You would not, of course, have lied to your host, would you?"

Lady Anne fixed her with that deadly glare again, and almost hissed, before swallowing sharply, and responding in a voice as treacle sweet as possible.

"Of course I would not do such a shocking thing! You must have misheard me, Lady Charity."

Charity did not deign to respond, simply indicating the door to the room where the necessary was located, and allowing Lady Anne to enter before her.

As she did, she glanced back down the hallway, to see Lady Chilwinth slipping back into the parlour – but not before she had looked at Charity with a baleful glare. It seemed that Lady Chilwinth had been on her way to 'discover' her daughter and the Duke.

She felt oddly pleased with herself, even though she knew that she had just made enemies – for Charity was not prone to courage, or to challenging others. That sense of pride in herself, for doing what was right even though she found it difficult, stayed with her for the rest of the day.

She noted, as the day became evening and she sat through dinner and the gathering in the parlour afterwards, that the Duke carefully avoided Lady Anne, and spent most of his time with his gentlemen friends.

*****

Rafe had, for the first moment when he had looked up from his desk as the door clicked open, felt a surge of positively gut-wrenching terror. As far as he knew, there was no one else anywhere near, and now, here was Lady Anne walking into his study. Then, just as he was considering simply bodily ejecting her at speed, and slamming the door shut, he saw Lady Charity beyond her, in the hallway.

His first thought, even as he asked Lady Anne what she was doing, was to wonder if Lady Charity would scream, and call compromise, if she was assisting Lady Anne in what seemed a very obvious attempt to trap him – but he was rapidly disabused of that notion. Lady Charity met his eyes – her violet ones wide and filled with a keen understanding of the situation.

Perhaps he was not doomed after all. Then, with very clear intention, Lady Charity knocked a side table against the wall. Lady Anne spun to look, her expression in that moment revealing all he needed to know of her plan. When Lady Anne turned back, she had schooled that expression.

Her words had been ingenuous at best – a poor attempt at prevarication – but Lady Charity had saved him, speaking up in a manner which left Lady Anne with no choice, making leverage of the poor excuse that Lady Anne had given.

Once the woman was out of the room, he had shut and locked the door, then sagged against it with relief.

His mother had been right to warn him of that one.

He would have to be far, far more careful than he had been. He had not expected such a blatant attempt, so soon, and he was quite certain that there would be other tries, perhaps far more subtle. It made it almost worth choosing one of the young women as fast as possible, just to remove the potential for one he disliked trapping him.

With that thought, came the image of Lady Charity, and her intelligent, concerned violet eyes. He remembered his thoughts, after his last discussion with his mother – might she be a suitable choice? Might the quiet, violet eyed woman be the wife he needed? He could not know – he had barely spoken to her.... yet... he obviously needed to do so again, preferably without others listening. And, if they were alone, without anyone else knowing - or the choice would be taken from him – not by Lady Charity, for he did not suspect her of any intent to trap him – but by anyone else who might discover them alone together.

Why did society's rules have to make this whole process so difficult?

*****

The following morning dawned clear, crisp, and cold, with a sharp frost coating everything in a sparkling lace of ice.

Charity woke with the dawn – not that dawn was especially early, in midwinter - and looked out of her window, finding delight in the glittering landscape. Overhead, a flock of seabirds wheeled, their cries coming to her on the light breeze. It was a perfect morning for a walk.

She called for Maggie, dressed warmly, took up her basket, and slipped down the servants' stairs to escape the house unseen by any guests. Not, she thought, that most of them were likely to rise for another few hours anyway, not if they kept the usual hours of the *ton*.

She relaxed once she was past the stables, and away down the lane, although she was sorely tempted to slip into the stables first, just to talk to the horses. Riding was something she loved, and she missed her mare, Kestrel, when they were away – but today, going into the stables carried too much risk of being seen, and that would prevent her from having this walk, alone.

She hoped that those seabirds had been kind enough to shed some feathers for her – or perhaps she would find more prosaic specimens caught on the hedge, or lying, frost drenched, under the trees at the edge of the fields further on. She needed more feathers – perhaps even a visit to the Oakmoor home farm to seek out chicken feathers would be worth it. Some types of chicken had truly stunning feathers, especially the roosters. If she did that, of course, she would have to take Maggie with her, for propriety.

The lane yielded no feathers until well past the bend where she had first met the Duke, but when she did find some, it was an excellent find – a cluster of feathers of varying size, scattered in the way that suggested a bird had met its fate at the teeth of a fox. She gathered them up, smoothing them and settling them carefully into her basket – even the tiny downy ones.

Once she was sure that she had them all, she went on, discovering a stile which allowed access through the hedge, and onto the long rolling fields which ran down to the sea cliffs. She climbed it, and studied the land ahead - she had not intended to walk so far, yet the thought of the view from those cliffs drew her. She set off, studying the ground as she went, as ever, on the hunt for feathers.

*****

Rafe had risen early, and set out to walk – he needed to clear his head with the crisp morning air, to escape the cloying scents of too much perfume which seemed to have filled the house, and to have a space in which he might be alone, without risk of being manipulated into a trap by Lady Anne. He was quite, quite certain that she would still be abed for some hours.

He took his usual path, past the far end of the formal garden, down the lane towards the home farm, and then out onto the fields, and down to the cliffs. Above him, the gulls soared, wheeling and diving as always. As he stepped away from the lane, something bright caught his eye.

A feather.

Caught on a scraggly low bush.

He bent, and carefully extracted it from the twigs, then tucked it into the front of his coat, where his waistcoat might hold it flat and protected. He smiled at his own whimsy – what was he going to do with that feather? The image of Lady Charity rose in his mind, and he shook his head – would he give it to her? But that would look far too much like he was favouring her. He walked on, with it still tucked against his heart. Perhaps, later...

Ahead, the glow of the sun rising lit the edge of the cliffs, and made the fields before him seem paved in gold. Whimsy definitely had taken hold in his thoughts this morning! He squinted slightly against the glare of the sun as it slipped above the line of the cliffs – was that something out of place? For there seemed to be a silhouette, lit by that glare, where he knew, for a certainty, that there were no trees.

He walked faster, curious now, and as the sun rose a little higher, no longer casting sharp stars of glare off the cliff edge, he realised that the silhouette was a person, walking, as he was, towards the cliffs. A woman, in fact, coming from the direction of the stile at the end of the stables' lane. He studied her as he walked, for something about her seemed familiar. Then, she paused, and bent to the ground, as if she was picking up something. As she did, he noticed the small basket over her arm.

A smile covered his face – it was Lady Charity, he was almost certain – and she had just stopped to pick up a feather. He kept walking, feeling unaccountably more cheerful than he had moments before. He came up with her, when they were but scant yards from the cliff edge.

"Good morning, Lady Charity."

She started, and spun towards him.

"Your Grace! I did not hear you approaching."

"I did not plan to catch you unawares... but now that we are here, shall we take the last few steps, and watch the morning sun over the sea? I always find it a soothing sight."

She blushed, and nodded, then stepped forward. He moved beside her, fascinated, yet again. She had not simpered, or gushed at him about the view, or anything else he might have expected.

Soon, they stood close to the edge, the beach below them, where the waves tumbled stones, and the sun cast a path of light towards them across the sea. She spoke, hesitantly, and he turned to regard her.

"Your Grace... yes, it is beautiful. I like to come out early, by myself, scandalously improper as that is. For the early morning is peaceful, and does not require me to engage in pointless social conversation. Oh... I'm sorry, I didn't... I..."

She stopped and her faced reddened further.

"Do not worry, I am not offended – for I understood that you did not refer to our conversation here. And I agree with you, with respect to pointless social conversation. There are moments when I think that the majority of my houseguests have not a thought in their heads beyond the weather, and the best colour for a bonnet - and whether they might become my Duchess, by fair means or foul. Thank you for what you did for me, yesterday. Without your intervention, I have no doubt that I would have been faced with Lady Chilwinth, crying 'compromise', within minutes."

"Indeed you would have been – for I saw her, after you had closed the door, slipping back into the parlour – she was but moments away from the door of your study."

"Then I am doubly grateful to you, Lady Charity."

She blushed again as he met her eyes. Such beautiful eyes. So expressive. He was caught for a moment, entranced.

"You need not thank me, Your Grace – I did only what any reasonable person would do. In truth, I had heard Lady Anne and Lady Chilwinth whispering, earlier, discussing the fact that, as you had not shown any preference for Lady Anne, they would take more drastic action. I was horrified, but I had no way to warn you. So, when Lady Anne slipped from the parlour, not long after you had left the room, I made an excuse to leave the room also, and followed her. I had the most dreadful feeling..."

"And you were correct. Without your quick thinking, I would by now most likely have been forced into a betrothal with Lady Anne. Which is almost the worst fate that I can imagine."

He perhaps should not have been so blunt about that, he realised, as the words left his mouth, yet with this woman, absolute honesty seemed right – and she did not appear shocked at all by what he had said. Oddly, she looked a little surprised, and a small frown marred her brow.

"I would have thought..."

She stopped, and looked away, as if embarrassed to have spoken.

"What would you have thought, Lady Charity?"

Those violet eyes met his again.

"May I be blunt, Your Grace?"

"Of course, Lady Charity. In general, I prefer honesty and forthrightness to insinuation and simpering."

She blinked, this time truly looking shocked.

"Your Grace, I would have thought that a lady such as Lady Anne – but one who was not attempting to trap you – with her good breeding, polished appearance and accomplishments, would have been exactly what a Duke would look for, in his Duchess."

Her words startled a laugh from him, and she almost flinched at the sound. He reached out, without conscious thought, to touch her arm in reassurance.

"I do believe that my mother would agree with that statement. But I do not. If I must marry, and get an heir, I would like to marry a woman I can talk to, of far more than weather and fashion. A woman who I might actually like, or even love, and who might care for me, as a person, not just for the title and wealth that marrying me would bring her. My mother would call me a hopeless romantic for those words, and decry me as impractical. Yet still, that is how I feel."

Chapter Five

Charity felt almost dizzy.

The Duke's words resonated within her, deep into her bones, for they rang with truth and sincerity. He truly felt as he had just described. But the fact that he was unimpressed with the likes of Lady Anne did not make him more likely to be impressed with Charity, she reminded herself.

She was plain, and awkward, she blurted out her thoughts entirely too easily – she would make a dreadful Duchess. And, anyway, whilst the Duke seemed very comfortable talking to her, she was sure that he saw her as a sort of friend, rather than as a woman to consider for his wife. His manner contained nothing of courtship at all.

But, she realised, she would be happy to have this man as a friend, even if that was all that she might have. Perhaps, if he often walked early... they might meet again, here, where they could talk, without being overheard? Which thought reminded her that she was alone with him, unchaperoned.

"Your Grace... that is most... unusual of you. But... I must ask – are you not concerned about me – about us being here, alone, together?"

He turned those deep brown eyes on her again, and his lips curved into a smile

"Lady Charity, it is usually a lady who feels concerned about being found alone with a gentleman, concerned about her reputation. So I should ask you the same – are you not concerned?"

Charity felt her cheeks heat yet again – somehow, he made her blush, without ever making her feel belittled.

"I... Your Grace, I find that I have no fear of you. I find you an honourable man, and I trust that you will do nothing improper. And... I will admit that I enjoy speaking with you, at least here, when I need not worry about how anyone else will interpret my words."

"Thank you for your faith in me, Lady Charity. In return, I offer my belief in you – I trust that you have no plans to entrap me, and that you will speak honestly with me, without guile or deceit. And that is something which I greatly appreciate."

It was true, Charity thought – she had no plans to entrap him – even though her mother desperately hoped that he might pay her attention. Which seemed very, very unlikely, after this conversation. It felt as if she had just been offered friendship, with the caveat that it could never become anything more.

"Thank you for believing me honest, Your Grace. I must admit that my mother has often despaired of my directness, for I find it most difficult to speak in the manner of much of the *ton*, with layers of meaning and implication. It is refreshing to meet someone who values that directness."

He met her eyes again, and she felt herself drowning in his gaze. He smiled, and he was so very handsome when he did – she could understand the desire of every young woman at this house party, to tempt him.

"Despite our agreement on such matters, Lady Charity, I feel that you have raised a very good point. The morning is moving on apace, and we are out here, in rather plain view of anyone who should gaze across the fields towards the cliffs. Our unchaperoned state would definitely cause some drama, should we be seen. Therefore, I suggest that we both proceed back towards the house, by separate paths – I would suggest that, as you came via the stables' lane, you go back via the home farm lane, and I do the opposite. That way, should anyone notice us coming back, we will arrive from different directions."

"That sounds most sensible, Your Grace."

He took her hand for a moment, and Charity felt her heart pound hard within her breast as he bowed over it, elegantly.

"I have enjoyed our little moment of peace, Lady Charity. Should I happen to come upon you another day, out walking in the very early morning, I believe that would be most pleasing. For now, farewell."

He turned and walked away, leaving Charity a little stunned, and considering his words. Had he... had he really just suggested... Yes, she rather thought that he had.

Despite her belief that he intended only friendship, the thought made her happier than she had felt for years.

*****

Rafe took his time about going back – his mother could be as annoyed as she wished, but he would not spoil the morning by hurrying. He walked the longer path, not via the stile into the lane, but around the copse of trees where the lane ended, and along the fields on the other side until he reached the far side of the stables' buildings. By the time he arrived there, another three feathers had joined the first, tucked under his waistcoat.

He wondered idly what Lady Charity did with feathers – and why being aware of her interest in them made him notice every single one that he passed. He supposed that her purpose was irrelevant, so long as she obtained pleasure from collecting them. He discovered that he wanted to present her with the ones he had found, to see if her face lit with that smile of happiness he had seen for a few moments as she watched the sun on the sea.

But how he might achieve such a thing was a question for which he had no answer.

He walked through the main stable, pausing to greet his stallion, Valiant, on his way through. The grooms paid him no heed, being used to his wanderings, and knowing that, if he required anything of them, he would ask. The scent of horses and leather surrounded him, and he was hard pressed to make himself leave it, to return to the house, and the perfumes which he had come to think of as the scent of greed and opportunism.

But he had his duty, he was a man of his word, and there was no escaping it – he had made a vow.

As he strode into the house, the pressure of the small bundle of feathers against his heart was oddly reassuring.

*****

The next two days brought rain – icy rain which was very nearly sleet – and all houseparty activities were, of necessity, constrained to the house. Charity felt completely trapped, for she could not spend all day in her rooms, yet when she ventured into the parlour, Lady Anne was waiting, and singled her out, drawing Charity into conversations where she could mock her in subtle ways. Ways which were getting less and less subtle, the longer Charity managed to appear to ignore them.

The only thing which had lightened her days had been the moment, yesterday, when she had been walking along the Long Gallery, admiring the paintings of the Duke's ancestors in the rather watery light which came through the tall windows which lined one side of the room, and had discovered, on a window ledge, a feather. It seemed a very strange place to find one, but she supposed that it was possible that a bird had come in, when the windows had been open on a day with less inclement weather.

She had gathered it up with a smile, gently stroking it flat, and tucked it away in the pockets of her day gown.

Today, there had been no such bounty and, after a morning spent in the library, her mother had insisted that she join everyone else in the parlour. She had tried to slip into the bay window seat, and simply read, but almost as soon as she had moved in that direction, Lady Anne, and the other young women who tended to spend their time with her, had descended.

"Dear Lady Charity, do join us! We were just discussing the merits of being outgoing, compared to being more reclusive."

Miss Woodfield looked at Charity, and smiled – a smile reminiscent of a cat who had just trapped a bird beneath its paw. Charity forced herself not to shiver, and simply waited for whatever they might say next. Miss Woodfield spoke.

"And we thought to consult you, dear Lady Charity, for you are such a perfect example of the reclusive..."

Lady Anne tittered, and gave Charity a look which threatened, even whilst being camouflaged as sweetness.

"And I, of course, stand on the side of being outgoing. I cannot imagine how dull it must be, to hide away all the time, like a mouse. How do you bear the tedium?"

Charity forced herself to consider carefully before she answered.

"There is no tedium to bear, Lady Anne, when one is clever enough to amuse oneself."

Lady Anne looked at her, obviously shocked, and for just a moment, Charity was proud of herself – not only had she not just blurted out her first thought, but she had managed to choose words which were the complete truth, yet still subtly suggested that Lady Anne was not very intelligent. Miss Woodfield looked interested, as if she had not expected Charity to be capable of such a riposte. Then she spoke again.

"But Lady Charity, what is the point of amusing oneself, alone? That most certainly is not likely to attract the attention of a Duke... and surely, you are here for the same reason that all of us are..."

Charity swallowed, wishing desperately to escape them. To continue this conversation would test her to the utmost. She wanted simply to tell them, very impolitely, to leave her alone. Which of course was what they wanted – they desired to discompose her so badly that she would behave inappropriately in front of everyone. She lifted her eyes for a moment, and discovered, to her horror, that the Duke stood a very short distance away, and was observing the interchange closely.

Lady Anne and the others could not see him, for he was behind them. He… she was quite sure that he winked at her. Shock filled her, and Lady Anne spoke again, obviously displeased by her silence.

"Lady Charity, did you hear what Miss Woodfield said? Do tell me – you are here in the hope of attracting the attention of the Duke, aren't you? Although it seems most unlikely, that you could achieve that, surely that is why you are here?"

Irritation filled Charity, and all thought of restraining her response departed her.

"I am here because I was invited to this house party, Lady Anne. That, and nothing more. Should the Duke consider me worth spending time with, so be it, but I have no intention of attempting to influence him in any way. Such manipulation is beneath a lady of quality."

It was far too bluntly spoken – shockingly so, and Lady Anne's face made that abundantly clear to her. Behind Lady Anne, the Duke was still watching, his expression one of amusement.

"How… how dare you imply… you dreadful chit. I should…."

"What should you do, Lady Anne?"

The Duke's voice was low, richly resonant. He stepped up to stand in a position where Charity was to one side of him, and Lady Anne the other. His expression now was one of polite interest, and Charity envied him the ability to be so calm. Lady Anne almost spluttered, desperately trying to school her face to an expression of simpering delight at his presence, rather than the somewhat ferocious look she had turned on Charity moments before.

"Ah… I… Your Grace."

Lady Anne curtsied and the Duke smiled, a socially polite smile, which might cover thoughts a great deal different in nature. It was, Charity thought, so very much in contrast to the genuine smile he had given her, that morning on the sea cliffs.

"Yes, Lady Anne?"

"I was just commenting, Your Grace, that I should thank you for hosting this delightful house party."

Charity barely managed to keep her expression bland – the gall of Lady Anne! And the foolishness of her – did she really think that the Duke would be so easily deceived? Apparently, she did.

The Duke considered her for some moments, as the silence stretched, and Lady Anne began to look uncomfortable – the simpering smile on her face becoming a little less so.

"I see. Then you had best thank my mother, as she is the one who has organised all of... this." He waved his hand as if to include everything around them, "Personally, I often find such events somewhat dull, no matter how hard my mother tries to ensure that everyone is entertained."

Lady Anne gaped at him, then quickly restored the false smile to her face. He had as much as implied that she was dull, without ever needing to say so. Her eyes narrowed, and her lips compressed, before she caught herself, and restored that supposedly charming smile again.

"How sad for you, Your Grace. I will do as you say, and thank your mother – but... is there no way in which I might... make the party more entertaining... for you...?"

Charity blinked, stunned at how blatant and improper that question was.

She took the opportunity to carefully move away from the conversation, whilst everyone's attention was focussed on Lady Anne. She slipped back, and then turned, planning to go to her mother's side.

As she did, she heard the Duke's reply – still spoken calmly, but with steel in his tone.

"Lady Anne, I do not believe that there is anything... anything at all... that you could possibly do which would achieve your aim. Do not waste your effort – I am sure that there are far better things you could turn your energies to. And now, forgive me, ladies, but I must speak with some of my other guests."

Charity kept moving towards her mother, who stood near the fire, chatting with the Duchess. She hoped that Lady Anne had understood the Duke's meaning, and would cease her attempts to trap him – but she was not, truly, hopeful of that. The woman was determined, and remarkably unpleasant. But what had the Duke thought – what had he meant by that wink?

She did not know, but at least he had broken up the conversation before Lady Anne could attack Charity more than she already had – and Charity suspected that he had done so on purpose, to help her. The idea of that made her feel warm inside.

She reminded herself, yet again, that he was unlikely ever to regard her with more than friendship. Saving her from Lady Anne just now was simply his way of repaying her for saving him from the woman a few days earlier. Nothing more. She must keep that truth in mind at all times, lest she foolishly hope for more than she could reasonably expect

*****

Rafe felt anger slice through him like a knife, bringing a cold sharp edge to his thoughts. He was not a man who grew hot headed with anger – rather, he became cold, calculating, and precise. Lady Anne drove that anger to a fierce pitch. He had heard every word of that conversation – a conversation specifically designed to attack Lady Charity, and to provoke her to respond without thought, out of hurt.

He had been deeply impressed by the way in which Lady Charity had managed – given what she had told him, out there on the sea cliffs, about her tendency to directness. But he had known that she needed help, when she had made that declaration about her purpose for being here – that had been blunt enough to indicate that she was distressed indeed.

He needed, now that Lady Charity had escaped Lady Anne and her cohort, to escape them himself. He would ask his gentlemen friends to the billiards room – a location to which Lady Anne was unlikely to dare to follow. But… part of him would have preferred to stay, to seek out Lady Charity, and make sure that she was not further distressed.

He could not allow himself to do that, however – it would single her out, and make her even more of a target for Lady Anne and her friends – which he would never wish to do. He must simply hope that the morrow dawned clear, and that she might venture out. If he met her on the fields again… then, perhaps he could express his concern.

Chapter Six

Charity woke early, and lay there, as the pre-dawn light filtered through the slightly open curtains. After a moment, she pushed the covers back, and went to the window, peering through the gap in the curtains. The day looked clear – no rain or snow, and no wind.

She turned away, and rang for Maggie. It was the perfect sort of morning to walk, especially after two days of rain. As Maggie did up the annoying row of small buttons on her gown, Charity considered what she would do – should she walk to the cliffs again? Or actually go to see the stables? Or perhaps the home farm? She weighed up the options, and decided to do two of those things – to visit the stables, and indulge in a few minutes of seeing horses, before slipping out along the lane towards the cliffs again.

"Maggie... will you come down with me? I want to go to the stables – I miss Kestrel so. But to go there, I need you, for propriety. After that, I will slip away for my normal walk, and you can come back up here."

“Of course, my Lady. Your mother won’t wake for quite some time yet, so I should be back by the time that she needs me. I’ll just get my coat.”

Charity slipped her pelisse on, and gathered up her basket. Maggie soon returned, and they went out, down the servants’ stairs, and across to the stables.

There was some activity there, as the grooms and stableboys went about their business, mucking out stalls, refilling haynets and water buckets, and doling out morning feeds. They looked at her curiously, but did not object to her presence. She walked down the long line of stalls, pausing occasionally to hold her hand out for curious horses to sniff, before running her gloved fingers down their faces in greeting, or scratching just above the eye ridge, where most horses loved to be touched.

Maggie hung back near the doors, just watching her, content to let her wander. The maid had known her a long time, and knew that she was most competent around horses. Towards the far end of the long building, Charity stopped before the stall of a mare whose blood bay coat was a close match for the tone of Charity’s own hair. The mare was magnificent – well conformed, her coat gleaming. She turned, a mouthful of hay dangling, and eyed Charity for a moment before stepping across the large stall to stretch her head over the stall door to sniff at Charity.

Charity held out her hand, relaxed, and stood still as the mare inspected her. When she did nothing more, the mare nudged her hand with her nose, and Charity, laughing, obeyed the command, and caressed her face, then scratched gently about her ears, and the ridge above her eye. The mare leant into her touch.

“I see that you are used to horses, Lady Charity. Sage seems rather taken with you, and she won’t talk to everyone.”

Charity started, her hand falling back to her side – a situation which was greeted by another firm nudge from the mare.

"Your Grace! I did not hear you approach. You seem to have a talent for taking me unawares."

He laughed, and the warm rich tone of it made her quiver inside.

"I do not mean to!"

Sage nudged her again, and Charity automatically reached for her, caressing, even though her eyes still rested on the Duke.

"She is beautiful, Your Grace – all of these horses are, but this one – Sage – really caught my attention. She reminds me of my own mare..."

"Ah, so you ride? So many ladies rarely do, preferring carriages. Do you ride... energetically? Or are you more prone to a gentle wander about the countryside?

"Your Grace, are you asking me if I am useless on a horse – are you attempting to politely discover if I actually ride, or simply let the horse carry me about at a walk?"

As she said it, Charity felt herself blush again. There she was, being too direct, as always. What if he was offended? But he smiled – that devastating smile which made him look handsome beyond belief, and laughed again.

"Lady Charity, I am so used to having to be delicate with my phrasing, lest I offend one of those fragile flowers of the *ton*, that I quite forget that there are women capable of directness. I find your forthrightness delightfully refreshing."

Charity met his eyes, stunned, wondering for a moment if he could possibly be serious. There was nothing but sincerity in those deep brown eyes.

"Oh. Well... that makes you a most unusual man, Your Grace."

"I find myself flattered by that statement. And yes, Lady Charity, I suppose I was attempting to ask you about your level of skill as a rider."

"I... my mother would berate me for being too proud – but yes, I am a good rider. I am more like to ride in a manner not too dissimilar to that in which I speak – to launch myself into things before putting much careful thought into it. I have, therefore had to learn to ride well, if only to save myself successfully from the scrapes I get myself into. Mother long ago refused to watch me ride, lest I give her too many new grey hairs. She is more the type who prefers a sedate walk through the countryside."

She was babbling – she knew it, and what had she said! Oh, now he would think her foolish! But he laughed again – a full bodied sound of genuine delight, and she felt the blush rise in her cheeks.

"Wonderful! Then... as Sage seems rather taken with you – would you like to ride her?"

Charity did not stop to think, as usual – the words came tumbling from her mouth.

"Oh, thank you, Your Grace – I would very much like that! I have been missing my mare, missing my rides."

"I was just about to ride, as it happens – I do so almost as many mornings as I walk. Would you like to come with me – accompanied by a groom, of course, for propriety?"

For a moment, Charity felt her heart lift with joy. Then, almost as fast, that joy came crashing down.

She did not have a riding habit with her.

Her mother had not expected there to be any chance of her riding, and had told Maggie not to pack it. She felt, in that instant, close to tears. Sage nudged her again, instinctively knowing, as horses did, that she was unhappy. She caressed the mare, grateful for her sympathy.

"Your Grace… I would be absolutely delighted to… if I could. But… I do not have a riding habit with me. I did not expect…"

*****

Rafe had been startled when he had walked into the stables, and seen Lady Charity there. He had followed her down the row of stalls, coming up to her as she stopped at Sage's stall. The mare was kind, but strong willed, and a good judge of character – he had seen her snap at people whose character he knew to be less than ideal, as often as he had seen her seek to be touched and spoken to by those who were more kind by nature.

As he watched, the mare demanded attention from Lady Charity, who gave it with every evidence of pleasure. So focussed was she on the horse that she quite jumped when he spoke to her.

And now, after an exchange which was as unusual as every exchange with Lady Charity seemed to be, he had rashly asked her to ride with him – which was not at all the way to avoid making it seem as if he singled her out for his attention! She had instantly looked delighted – and he could not crush that delight – he would simply have to deal with the reactions of the others.

But, just as he was about to speak again, her face crumpled into misery, and she spoke, her voice far softer.

"Your Grace... I would be absolutely delighted to... if I could. But... I do not have a riding habit with me. I did not expect..."

His first thought was *'well, that should be easy to resolve, my mother is a slim woman, not too different in size from Lady Charity – surely she will have a habit that Lady Charity might borrow'*. And that thought was immediately followed by the recognition that, should he ask his mother such a thing, she would instantly interpret it as meaning that Rafe was rather taken with Lady Charity...

He had just trapped himself. He had already asked her to ride with him, and he had seen how much she truly wanted to ride – he could not, simply could not, allow something so minor as a piece of clothing to prevent her from having that enjoyment. He would have to do it, would have to ask his mother.

"Lady Charity – whilst that does mean that you accompanying me this morning is not possible, I do not think that it is an insurmountable obstacle. I do believe that my mother may be able to assist you with a habit, which would allow you to join me on another morning. I will enquire of her, and let you know the answer."

She gasped, and met his eyes, her expression shocked. He was not sure why – he did not think that he had said anything truly out of place – a little unusual, perhaps... but... then that expression changed to a smile – a smile which lit her face and made her eyes sparkle.

"Your Grace, that is beyond kind of you. I will be more grateful than I can express, should it be possible. But now, I am keeping you from your ride. I will just spend a little more time with Sage, then go for a walk. Enjoy your ride – may it give you a sense of peace to carry into the day."

He bowed, pleased, and stepped away, calling to a nearby groom to bring Valiant out and saddle him. No matter what his mother might think, it would be worth it, if he could bring that sort of smile to Lady Charity's face again.

*****

Charity watched him walk away as the mare lipped at her bonnet ribbons, hay scented breath blowing tendrils of her hair about. Absently, she gently pushed the mare away.

"No, Sage, you may not eat my bonnet, even if it is woven of straw!"

She walked slowly down the aisle of stalls again, back towards where Maggie waited at the door. Just outside that door, a groom held the chestnut stallion he had just led out, and the Duke stepped up to him, then swung effortlessly to the saddle. She envied him – envied the freedom that men had, to move about in breeches, to so easily ride whenever they wished to, no chaperone required.

Not that she found sidesaddle tiresome – far from it – for she was most comfortable doing almost anything that way – when that is the way you have always ridden, it is completely natural – but... she would not, ever, admit to anyone that she was curious about what riding astride might feel like...

She shook her head – it was time to walk across the fields, to let the sharp morning air clear her head and to steel herself for the day ahead. She could not, absolutely could not, allow the hope of a possible riding habit, and a ride, to grow too large, or she would be all the more devastated if it did not come to pass. She stopped beside Maggie.

"I'll just walk out along the lane a bit, then maybe on the fields – but I won't be long – I've spent longer here than I should have."

"As you wish, Lady Charity. I think that the Duke must like you. He certainly smiled at you, whatever he said!"

"Oh Maggie, don't read anything into it. We just talked about horses, and he asked me if I enjoyed riding – that's all."

"Well, it's a good thing that you do, then, my Lady."

They stepped out onto the gravel of the stableyard as the Duke rode away down the lane. Charity set off in his wake, her eyes following him, her heart wishing that she was beside him, riding away from all of the complexity of dealing with Lady Anne, and the other young women.

Maggie went across to the kitchen-garden gate, and back towards the house.

Chapter Seven

Later that morning, Charity went downstairs, considering how best to deal with the day. Perhaps if she kept a book with her, and simply sat quietly and read, the other women would leave her alone. She asked a passing maid for the direction of the library, and the maid led her there immediately.

The Oakmoor Chase library was huge – bigger than any that Charity had ever before been in, and when the maid led her through the door, she stopped, stunned, taking in the vast collection of books before her.

"Good morning, Lady Charity."

She spun towards the voice – it was the Duke. He had done it again, startling her, appearing where she did not expect him to be.

"Good morning, Your Grace."

"Are you seeking a book to read, Lady Charity?"

"I am, Your Grace. I find myself tired of the ladies' conversation."

She knew that he would understand what she meant, and that belief was confirmed when he smiled.

“Then by all means feel free to select any book you wish to read. I can sympathise with your... tiredness... when it comes to the conversation we have experienced of late.”

Behind her, the maid still stood in the doorway, ensuring that propriety was served, for which Charity was most grateful.

“Thank you, Your Grace. I am... rather overwhelmed by the number of books you have here!”

“My father, and my grandfather, collected books obsessively, and I have continued to add to the collection. If you prefer novels, you will find them on the shelves just past the window. I will leave you to browse.”

With that, he turned towards the door, and the maid stepped back out ahead of him. Charity was already moving towards the shelves he had indicated, wondering just how many stories there might be, here, which she had not read. She heard the door close, and a deep silence surrounded her. there was only the gentle crackle of the fire in the grate, and the delightful scent of books.

Near an hour later, when the clock on the mantel struck one, she shook herself out of her absorption in the novel in her hands, and turned towards the door, tucking the book into the pockets of her day gown. Her mother would be annoyed – she should have been in the parlour long since. She crossed the room, and as she neared the door, something bright caught her eye, lying on the rich deep piled rug.

It was a feather. A beautiful iridescent feather, in reds and green gold shimmer, the like of which one found on the best roosters.

She bent to pick it up, running its soft length through her fingers. She was quite sure that it had not been there when she had entered the room. So – where had it come from?

Carefully, she tucked it into her pocket, settling it between the pages of the book, so that it would be held flat. All the while, she considered that question – where could it possibly have come from? Feathers did not just appear, by magic, on the perfectly maintained carpet of a room in a Ducal residence. Or, she thought, remembering the feather on the window ledge in the gallery, anywhere else in a house like this. Someone must have dropped it – accidentally? Or on purpose?

Which led to the question – who?

And there was only one possible answer, given that she was certain that it had not been there when she entered the room.

The Duke.

Her heart pounded and her mouth went dry – for... why would the Duke be carrying a feather, and why would he leave it here? Perhaps... so that Charity would find it?

If that was the case, it left her confounded. Yet... no one else here, except the Duke, her mother and Maggie, knew that she collected feathers. That he might care enough – that he had even remembered... warmth filled her, and a seed of deeply foolish hope took root in her heart.

*****

Rafe had waved the maid out ahead of him, then, as he turned to pull the door closed, he slipped a hand into his waistcoat, and pulled out the first feather his fingers came into contact with, and dropped it to the floor.

There were now ten feathers in a small bundle, tucked away on his person – ten feathers gathered over the days since he had first plucked that white feather from the hedge. He was a fool, but he simply could not help himself. It was like a child's game – he could not publicly give them to her, but he could leave them where she would find them.

Would she suspect? And, did it matter if she did?

He found that he didn't care. If the feathers made her happy, then he would continue to play this game. And, after nuncheon had been served for those who partook in such things, he would take his mother aside, and ask about the riding habit.

*****

The conversation in the parlour had been tedious, and he wished that he might have stayed in the library with Lady Charity, but, finally, everyone was beginning to settle into activities for the afternoon. He went to his mother, and spoke quietly to her, asking that she accompany him to his study. She raised an eyebrow, obviously curious, but said nothing as she moved towards the door.

As they left the room, Lady Charity entered it, and her face flushed when she saw him. Had she found it? He could not ask. Then she was past them, and the door closed on her. He did not speak until they reached his study.

"Well, Rafael, what is it that you wish to speak to me of, which requires privacy?"

He swallowed, knowing that his next words would create a strong reaction.

"I… have a request to make of you, Mother."

"A request? How interesting – please, do explain."

Rafe took a deep breath – he had committed to this, and he would do it, even knowing what his mother would think.

"I… I want you to loan Lady Charity one of your riding habits. I have discovered that she likes to ride, but has not brought a riding habit with her. You are not so dissimilar in size… I… I have invited her to ride with me – with a groom attending, of course, for propriety's sake."

For a moment, his mother met his eyes, her face a picture of stunned surprise, then her normally controlled manner slipped back into place.

"I take it that I should not enquire too closely into how you came by the information that she rides, and that she does not have a habit with her? Or into just when you might have been in a position to offer this invitation – which I assume, no one else knows about?"

Rafe felt suddenly just as he had as a boy, when she had caught him doing things he really should not.

"Indeed, I would prefer that you did not make those enquiries."

She studied him, and he thought, for a moment, that she would refuse his request – but she did not. Instead, a broad smile lit her face.

"There is hope yet, just when I had begun to despair. Yes, I will take her aside quietly, when everyone goes up to change for dinner, and find a habit which might fit her – either one of mine, or one of Mercy's which is still here."

"Thank you, Mother."

She waved the thanks away, and Rafe could tell that, just as he had expected, she had concluded that he had developed some true interest in Lady Charity. He paused, considering that – had he? He was shocked to discover that he no longer knew the answer to that question.

"Go back to your guests, Rafael – I will be back down shortly, after I set Mina looking through my old habits, and bringing them out."

He bowed, and left the room, feeling most pleased with the way that had gone – even if she was as likely to interrogate him about it later.

*****

Charity spent the afternoon in the parlour, mostly staying close to her mother, and avoiding any conversation with the other young women. Lady Anne cast her the occasional venomous glance, but, whilst she was near her mother, made no attempt to approach. They stood not far from the fire, and after a short while, the Duke returned to the room, and circulated amongst the guests, scrupulously avoiding spending too long with any one woman.

Charity watched him from under lowered lashes, unable to help herself, fascinated by how easily he seemed to navigate the treacherous waters of social conversation. He seemed almost a different man from the one she had spoken with so honestly, on the fields, or in the stable. Eventually, he came to them, in his rounds of the room. He greeted her mother, and bowed to her, the picture of propriety, then leant casually against the end of the mantel as her mother expounded on how much she was enjoying the house party.

Charity made noises of agreement when required, and he caught her eye, his filled with amusement – she knew, instantly, that he was quite aware that she was simply 'being good' for her mother. She looked away, blushing.

He finished that snippet of conversation, then bowed, saying that he must move on, and speak to others. He turned, and appeared to bump the arrangement of dried flowers which graced the mantel – he reached up, settling it back into place, and moved away. For once, Charity's eyes did not follow him. They were, instead, fixed on that flower arrangement – amongst which there now resided a feather – a feather which, most definitely, had not been there before.

It was him, she was sure, he had just, by some sleight of hand, put that feather there, even as she watched! But... she had no idea how she might retrieve it. She would manage, somehow – even if she needed to creep down here in the depths of the night.

As she contemplated that, the Duchess approached them. Around them, others were leaving the room, going up to change for dinner, and to rest a little before the evening's entertainments. Her mother spoke to the Duchess for a moment, then went to another of the older ladies to accompany her to the conservatory, where they had previously agreed to spend some time before going up. Charity had cried off from that, insisting that she would prefer to retire to her rooms, and rest there.

As she went to curtsey, and take her leave of the Duchess, the older woman put a hand on her arm to still her.

"Lady Charity, might I ask you to accompany me? I believe that you are in need of a riding habit?"

Charity regarded her, startled, then gave a nod.

"Yes, Your Grace."

"Then do come with me now, so that we might address that need." The Duchess led her from the room, and along a hall away from the main stairs to a smaller staircase. "These stairs lead directly to the family apartments – so much easier than winding through the upper halls."

They went up, and Charity looked about her, fascinated by this insight into the private life of the Duke and his family. The portraits which lined the upper hall they emerged into were older, and of more intimate family settings, the furniture surrounding them also older, and burnished to a rich sheen. They stopped before a large door, and the Duchess pushed it open.

"Mina!"

A maid scurried out when the Duchess called.

"Yes, Your Grace. I have four possible options laid out in the dressing room." Her gaze turned to Charity. "If you would come this way, my Lady?"

Charity went forward, and the Duchess accompanied her. In the dressing room, which was larger than her own bedroom at home, there were four riding habits, each laid out over a clothes-stand. They were made of beautiful fabrics – fine woven wools, rich velvets, and the like. They were far richer than the plain but serviceable habit which lay in her armoire at home.

The maid assisted her to remove her gown, and then to try on each of the habits in turn. All could be said to fit her, but one did so far better than the others. It was made in the finest woven wool that Charity had ever seen, with a jacket in the military style, the lapels of which were velvet. The whole was in shades of a deep burgundy, which, when she viewed herself in the mirror, seemed to make the deep red of her hair glow.

She had never worn something so wonderful before.

The Duchess regarded her, then turned to some shelves, and came back with a hat – a hat which used the same velvet in its trim, and was dressed with but two feathers, pinned in place with a sparkling diamond brooch. The feathers were white, and the effect, against the dark velvet, was stunning.

"There, Lady Charity – that will suit nicely. I do believe that it fits you perfectly. It was my daughter's – but it never suited her half as well as it suits you – which is why she left it here when she married. If you like it, please keep it – it will be my pleasure to know that it will be used, after all these years. Now let us get you back into your day gown. Mina will pack this up, and deliver it to your maid whilst we are all at dinner."

"Thank you, Your Grace… it is beautiful, you shouldn't…"

"Of course I should. Now don't quibble dear girl – just go and get ready for dinner."

Charity allowed herself to be dressed again, and obediently went out along the corridors back to her guest suite. But the image of herself, when seen in that mirror, stayed with her. She had looked, just for that moment, like a completely different person.

*****

The Duchess watched Lady Charity as she left the room, her face thoughtful. It seemed that her son had an excellent eye for a woman's figure! And, she suspected, also for a woman's character. If Lady Charity Pemberton was the one he ended up choosing, she would not be at all displeased.

She turned back into the dressing room, and as Mina packed the habit carefully into a clothing box, she selected gloves, a scarf, a necklace, and a bracelet, all of which went with the habit perfectly. If her son had singled out this young woman, if he cared enough to arrange a habit for her, then the Duchess would make certain that she shone. Not just as herself, but in a manner which utterly outdid every other young woman present.

For, even as it appeared her son did, she liked Lady Charity – which was more than she could say for any of the other young ladies at the house party.

*****

Rafe found dinner tedious, especially as he was seated next to Lady Anne. When everyone retired to the parlour for cards, rather than the gentleman and ladies going to separate rooms, he was very glad to rise from the table. And to remain as far from Lady Anne as he possibly could, from then on.

Once in the parlour, his eyes went to the dried flower arrangement, and he grinned. The feather was gone. Casually, he walked over to the fireplace and leant against the mantel – which coincidentally placed him barely a foot from where Lady Charity stood with her mother, who chattered away to Baroness Delfanning. Barely turning towards him, Lady Charity spoke very softly.

"Your mother has provided a riding habit. Might we... tomorrow morning?"

"Definitely. At dawn."

His voice was equally soft.

Chapter Eight

Charity stepped into the warmth of the stables, her breath causing plumes of mist before her after the chill air of outside. She was nervous – not about riding, but about what the Duke would think, when he saw her in the beautiful habit – which had arrived in her room with not just the wonderful hat, but with gloves, jewellery, and a scarf too. The Duchess was very generous – Charity would not have been able to afford such an ensemble in the normal course of things.

She smoothed her fingers over the fabric, and walked towards where the Duke was just leading Sage out of her stall. She was already saddled and bridled.

"Good morning, Your Grace."

He looked up, realising that she was there only when she spoke. His eyes widened.

"Mother has done well. That suits you perfectly."

Charity smiled, relief flooding her.

He looked pleased, and his words felt genuine – that was not flattery, for the sake of it, but a simple statement of fact, as he saw it.

With this man, she realised, she need never fear for lies and empty words – he spoke honestly with her, as he had promised, that day out on the cliffs.

"Thank you."

Behind her, she heard the crunch of hooves on gravel, as the grooms brought the Duke's stallion around from the other building.

She turned as the Duke reached her, and walked with him to the doors, her hand resting on Sage's neck as she did. The mare turned her head and gently nudged Charity, then obediently walked on.

They stepped out into the faint light of the breaking dawn, and Charity studied the sidesaddle on the mare. It was a perfect fit on the mare's back, and was a beautiful piece of the saddler's craft, with a suede seat and intricately carved flaps.

A saddle of far higher quality than her own, at home.

She ran her fingertips over it, then adjusted the stirrup, before taking the reins from the Duke, and flipping them up over the mare's neck, preparatory to mounting.

"Do you wish a mounting block? Or a hand lift?"

Charity smiled as she looked at him.

"No thank you. I long ago learned to mount by myself – I have fallen often enough from being a little too adventurous, so I needed to be able to get back in the saddle, in the field. Of course, if a horse is very tall, I might need help – but Sage is of a perfectly reasonable size."

She checked that the girths were suitably firm, made some adjustments, and then lifted her left foot to the stirrup, before pushing up smoothly, her right leg passing between her left leg and the horse's body before she settled onto the seat, and lifted her right leg over the pommel. Once her skirts were adjusted to fall as they should, she accepted the riding whip which the Duke offered her. Not that she would need to use it for anything other than the gentle taps to indicate direction – a good rider never needed to apply excess force.

As she took it from him, their fingers brushed, and, even through their gloves, that touch felt as if heat seared her. She forced herself to ignore the sensation.

The Duke went to his stallion, and was soon mounted, just as a groom came out with a solid gelding, and mounted up.

"I will follow at a reasonable distance, Your Grace, so that I can see you, for propriety's sake, but you will have some privacy to talk as you wish. Call if you require me for anything."

"Thank you, Simms."

The Duke waved in the direction of the lane, and Charity urged Sage forward. The mare went willingly, with an eager bounce to her stride which said that she would love to run, but was far too well trained to do anything difficult. Charity shifted herself slightly, gently testing the feel of the mare, her sensitivity to the touch on the reins, to the subtle movements of weight on the saddle, and was very pleased with the responses. This horse was a true delight to ride.

She drew up alongside the Duke as they passed into the lane, and he turned to meet her eyes. There was warmth there, and pleasure in the moment. She could simply sink into that gaze, and forget everything else, should she permit herself to.

"I see that you were completely honest when you claimed yourself a skilled rider. You have an excellent seat, and a sensitivity, an awareness of the horse, which only comes from long experience."

"Thank you, Your Grace. Sage is a delight! She is so very responsive."

She could feel her cheeks heat in response to his praise – there were not many things that she excelled at, and therefore few chances in her life for praise. And few men would praise a woman for riding well – they were more like to praise beauty than more practical skills.

They rode on in companionable silence for some time, allowing the horses some time at the walk to warm up, before going any faster. As they turned the bend in the lane, the Duke glanced at her, and raised an eyebrow.

"Shall we move a little faster now?"

In answer, Charity urged Sage forward, and the mare did a perfect transition straight from the walk to a gliding canter. The Duke moved almost in perfect synchrony, and they flowed on down the lane. He was so close that she could have touched him.

"Can we go out onto the fields?"

"Of course, Lady Charity."

"Ahh... when I've walked here, I've used the stile – is there a gate? Or do we jump?"

She was pleased to see that he looked rather startled at her question – obviously, he had not expected her riding skill to extend to jumping something the height of the stile. She could not help it – she laughed, truly happy in that moment.

He grinned at her, but his voice was steady when he answered.

"There is a gate, not far past the stile. It's not a good stile to jump, for the lane is too narrow there to give the horse a decent approach."

"The gate then – I would not want to risk Sage by attempting a jump where there is inadequate lead in. Did I shock you, Your Grace?"

"Only a little. Every time I speak with you, you prove to me, again, that you are not a simpering fragile flower – and very glad of it I am."

"And I am glad that you are pleased by that, rather than horrified. It is an unusual response..."

They reached the gate, and he leant down from Valiant's back to open it, then shut it the same way once she was through. Charity looked across the rolling fields towards the sea, and a strange madness took her – she turned the mare and sent her forward in a gallop, feeling the wind pull curls of her hair free of the pins, but not quite stealing the hat from her head.

For the first time in her life, she was enjoying herself – with a man. A man who, she was quite certain, saw her only as a friend – for surely, so blunt and unconventional a woman as Charity could never be his choice for his Duchess. She should, therefore, not allow herself to come to care for him – but she suspected that, to some extent at least, it was too late – she already cared.

*****

The groom reached the gate just in time to see his master and the Lady set off at a blistering pace across the fields. Rafe glanced back, noted that the man was at least where he could see them, then turned all of his concentration to the woman ahead of him – rich dark red hair, a rich burgundy habit, on a rich blood bay mare – she looked spectacular. And he was going to have to do his damnedest if he hoped to catch up with her.

A kind of wild delight filled him, and he gave Valiant his head, the crisp winter air streaming past, and the ground disappearing beneath them as if they flew. It was a long time since he had given himself to speed this completely.

He did not catch her – not until she slowed as they approached the cliffs, and brought the mare back to a steady walk. As he came up beside her, she turned her face to him, alight with the same kind of wild joy he felt. She was, in that instant, stunningly beautiful – much more so than those carefully primped young women back at the house could ever be.

It struck him then, that, if he must choose one, from amongst those in his house at present, he would choose her, above all others. But... would she wish it? Any of the others, he knew would fall at his feet in an ecstasy of greedy delight if he chose them – but Lady Charity? He did not know what she would do, what she would want. She had not, at any time, shown any sign of wanting to be chosen. He had the horrible suspicion that she viewed him with nothing more than friendship – which, admittedly was more than many society weddings might boast of, between husband and wife.

But he had come to realise that he wanted more than that. He wanted this comfort, this ability to enjoy the moment, as he had with her, but he wanted love, as well.

It was a shocking thing for him to wish, and most of his gentlemen friends would mock him if they knew – but it was a truth he had to accept – this house party had proved it to him, even more than the preceding year had.

And he would not push marriage on her, if she did not truly wish it, although if he offered, he suspected that she would be made to accept, no matter what she wished – for his mother had mentioned that rumour had it that she needed to marry, due to her father's advanced age, and their financial circumstances. He did not wish to force her to anything.

She deserved far better than that, was worth far more than as simply a bargaining chip – she was worth being loved, properly.

He pushed the thoughts away, and focussed on the moment, on the light in her eyes, and the happiness in her face. Everything else could wait until later.

"That, Your Grace, was wonderful! Sage is so fast, it felt as if we were flying."

"Perhaps you were – perhaps horses are capable of magic."

Where had that whimsical conceit come from? It did not matter, for she laughed again – a sound so melodic and full of joy that he wanted to hear it again.

"Perhaps they are. I suppose that we should go back soon – but I can't say that I look forward to the day – I believe that Lady Anne has arranged for the afternoon to be a kind of musicale – probably so that she can demonstrate what she believes to be her superior musical skills. Oh! I shouldn't have said that, should I?"

"Most likely not... but it is the truth. The very idea makes me shudder – for they will all expect me to sit through every minute of it, and praise their abilities."

“A dreadful fate, Your Grace.”

He found that they shared a conspiratorial smile, and all unthinking, he reached out and touched her cheek as the two horses continued to walk along the clifftop path, tightly side by side. She took a sharp breath, and he allowed his hand to drop. What did she think of him, for that touch?

He looked out at the sea. The rising sun laid its path of gold over the waves, and the sea birds wheeled above it. He turned back to see her watching him.

“Let us, then, delay that dreadful fate – let us walk along the cliffs here for a little longer, before we make our way, more sedately than we came, back to the stables.”

She met his eyes, and nodded, then a mischievous smile curled her lips.

“I am sure that poor Simms will appreciate it.”

A wave of her hand indicated the groom, who only now approached them across the fields.

He laughed, and they allowed the horses to walk on.

Chapter Nine

By the time that they arrived back at the stables, the morning was advanced enough that Charity suspected that her mother might be awake – which meant that others could be, too. She slipped down from Sage, and spoke to the mare for a minute before handing her off to the grooms, who led her away to a well-deserved brushing and feed.

"Thank you for this morning's ride, Your Grace. I had best hurry inside, and prepare for the day."

"Thank you for your company, Lady Charity. Perhaps we might do this again, tomorrow, or the day after?"

"I would very much like that, Your Grace. Do let me know when..."

"I will."

He bowed, and she hurried away, worried now that one of the other young women might see her, in the riding habit, and enquire.

She slipped in through the servants' door and up the servants' stairs – the footmen and maids smiled as she went past – perhaps Maggie had been talking to them, and they understood Charity's desire to remain inconspicuous. She gained her rooms without meeting anyone, and Maggie called for her bath, and for a breakfast tray.

An hour and a half later she went downstairs, wearing a plain daygown, and with a book in her pockets. Hopefully, the parlour would not be crowded yet, and she might simply sit in the bay window seat and read. But that hope was to be denied.

Her mother sat on one side of the room, discussing the embroidery she held with the Duchess, and nearly all of the young ladies were present, although not all of their parents. They clustered in groups, and Charity wondered, for a moment, what they found to talk about. In one corner of the room, the Duke stood with his gentlemen friends. He appeared to be absorbed in conversation, but she had the oddest feeling that he was acutely aware of everything happening in the room.

She walked in, and caught her mother's eye, then went towards the bay window, still hoping to simply sit quietly. It was not to be. Halfway across the room, she was intercepted by Miss Woodfield, who was trailed by her sister, Lady Anne, and two other ladies.

"Lady Charity, I must ask you to resolve a debate between myself, and my sister."

"A debate, Miss Woodfield?"

"Yes, Lady Charity. The fact of it is that I believe that I saw you, very early this morning, attired for riding, and returning from the stables. My sister declares that it cannot have been you, for you would never have a riding habit of such rich colour and quality."

Charity swallowed, hard, and forced herself not to speak. Not only had they seen her, but they had managed to turn even so simple a thing as a riding habit into an insult. And a trap.

She could answer that it was indeed her – defending by doing so her ability to have something of that quality, but revealing that she had been slipping out to ride, or she could deny it, and basically confirm, by doing so, that her family was so paupered that she could never afford such a thing.

They waited, their faces bland, but their eyes filled with a predatory gleam. Charity considered, and then the same madness took her that she had felt that morning – a sense that, if she simply threw herself into the challenge before her, it would all magically end well. She drew herself up, and forced a smile to her face.

"Miss Woodfield, let me end your debate in one sentence. Your sister is mistaken, for yes, it was me that you saw."

With that, she brushed past them, in a manner which bordered on the unacceptably rude, and continued to the bay window seat. She may have just damned herself to future interrogation, but at least she had retained her pride. Behind her, she heard the buzz of their chatter. It seemed that they had not expected courage – well, that was reasonable – she was not renowned for courage.

She was, in fact, almost shaking. But she hid it, and settled onto the seat, pulling out her book, and pretending that they did not exist. It was a pretence which did not succeed for long. They followed her, standing around the window seat in a manner which enclosed her, and felt almost threatening.

"And why were you riding – and with whom?"

Lady Anne's voice was sharp, hard.

Charity breathed deeply, barely preventing herself from declaring baldly that it was none of Lady Anne's business. Instead, she gritted her teeth, and held her smile in place.

"Lady Anne, I do not believe that you are my guardian, or chaperone, to ask such things. I ride because I enjoy it, and the Duke was kind enough to allow me the use of one of his horses."

Lady Anne and the Misses Woodfield exchanged annoyed glances. Charity waited, wondering what their next ploy would be. Looking past them, she saw the Duke approaching. He spoke to others as he moved through the room, but she knew, as soon as she saw him, that he was coming to see what Lady Anne and her clique were saying to Charity. Knowing that made her feel warm inside, and safer.

"Surely you did not go out alone, Lady Charity! That would be most improper."

"She did not. I accompanied her, as did a groom, for propriety."

The Duke's voice was warm, and almost amused as he rather firmly pushed himself into their little circle. The young women fell back a little, with expressions ranging from shock, to disbelief, to outright envy. Lady Anne turned to him, and her face transformed into that false sweet smile which Charity had seen her use so often. How she could conceive that anyone believed her sweet was beyond Charity's comprehension, but she obviously did.

"Your Grace! That was most... gentlemanly of you. I also enjoy riding at times – perhaps we might put together a riding party? If you have horses available, of course? And... at a more... sociable hour of the day?"

Charity almost gasped at the woman's audacity.

The Duke regarded her rather as if she was an insect, found unexpectedly in his food. He took some time before speaking, and Lady Anne began to shift about as if suddenly aware of just how forward she had been.

The Duke met Charity's eyes for a moment, and it was immediately obvious that he had as little interest in Lady Anne's suggestion as Charity did. Equally, she knew that he was about to agree to it. Duty drove him, and to refuse would be even more impolite than Lady Anne had been in asking.

"Lady Anne, I believe that would be possible. It will depend on how many are interested, and their riding skill – for I do not have a large number of ladies' horses here. If you would consult with my mother with respect to when such an outing might fit into the plans, we can see what can be arranged."

Lady Anne simpered, and made glowing exclamations of delight, all of which the Duke greeted with a face which spoke strongly of boredom. Charity almost laughed at the sight.

Somehow, he shooed them away to speak to the Duchess. Once they were far enough away that they would not hear his words, he spoke softly to Charity.

"I gather that they somehow discovered that you had been riding this morning?"

"Yes, they saw me returning to the house."

"How unfortunate. But I am sure that we will manage – because I am quite certain that you ride better than any of them. If they hope to use this as a way to attract more of my attention, they will fail. Do not let them disturb you – I am quite aware of how mean and petty minded they are."

"Thank you, Your Grace."

His words left her feeling warmed through, for his faith in her ability was a rare gift. He took her hand and bowed over it, then turned to move away, to continue circulating amongst the guests. But as he did, something fluttered to the floor, shifted by the breeze of his movement. Charity bent to look.

A feather.

She lifted it, and slipped it into her book, her smile becoming wide, and genuine. It was him, leaving her feathers to find. What that might mean, she did not know, but she liked him all the more for it.

*****

The following day it rained again, and the rain turned to light snow in the evening. Charity claimed a megrim, and stayed in her rooms, working on a feathered brooch, and a new feathered pin for her mother's hats.

She simply could not face another day in the company of Lady Anne and her friends. The previous afternoon's musicale had been excruciating – none of the young ladies had any significant musical skill, and at least two of them sang so badly that it had left Charity feeling quite ill. The only advantage had been that her own limited ability at the pianoforte had seemed quite good by comparison.

The day went by peacefully, and she was considering whether she might have a chance to walk again in the morning, should the rain and snow have stopped, when her mother came to inform her that the riding party would occur in the middle of the day, tomorrow, assuming that the day was clear. For a moment, she considered extending her megrim.

But no – that would be to let them win. She would ride, and do so proudly, no matter what spitefulness they might attempt. If the Duke had faith in her abilities, then she should have that same faith herself.

That night, she slept fitfully, dreaming odd dreams of riding amongst a crowd of others, and suddenly being unable to do so with any skill at all, of falling, and being surrounded by the mocking laughter of Lady Anne. She was grateful, when Maggie woke her, that the riding party would not happen until later in the day – it would give her time to shake the sense of doom which the dream had left her with.

She took breakfast in her room, and read for some time, finding that the day dragged, with the prospect of having to ride amongst the other women looming over her. At least the Duke would be there too, even if she would not be able to talk to him in the manner that the morning ride had allowed. Finally, it was time to dress for riding, and just the act of donning the beautiful habit made her feel better, stronger, and more capable.

Her mother came to tell her that most of the ladies had already gathered in the parlour, and Charity rose and went out, ready to join them.

Her mother had asked her, quietly, the night after the incident in the parlour which had created this riding party, for the truth about the habit, her ride with the Duke, and how Lady Anne had heard of it. Charity had answered honestly, as she always did, and her mother had regarded her with a very odd expression, then simply nodded, and left her to sleep. Charity suspected that her mother was nurturing hope that the Duke would choose her – a hope which Charity was certain was in vain.

As soon as she stepped into the parlour, all eyes turned towards her.

Despite feeling most uncertain in the face of the judgemental looks she faced, Charity forced herself to smile. The Duke stood in his usual position near the fireplace. He met her eyes, and gave the tiniest of nods. It was enough to encourage her.

Then he spoke, raising his voice a little so that all could hear.

"Ladies and gentlemen, as we are all gathered and ready, let us proceed to the stables. My grooms should have the horses prepared by now."

As they began to move, Charity noted that only five of the other young women were attired for riding – some had apparently cried off from this entertainment – for which, she thought with some amusement, the Duke was likely most grateful, for where he might have produced ten or more sidesaddles from, she was not sure – that he could muster six was impressive in itself.

She allowed the crowd to sweep her along, seeking only to keep moving, but somehow, as they stepped out of the front door, she found the Duke beside her. A fact which earned her venomous glances from Lady Anne and Miss Woodfield. She ignored them, confident that they would not do anything outrageous when the Duke walked so close to her.

At the stables, a row of grooms waited, each holding a saddled horse. As soon as they arrived, Simms came to her, leading Sage. She ignored the others, and concentrated on the mare, greeting her with a scratch on the eye ridge, and then checking the girths, and the stirrup. She mounted with her usual ease, Simms handed her the whip, and only then, once comfortably settled on the mare, did she look at what was occurring around her. It was almost, but not quite, chaos. She stifled laughter.

The Duke was going from lady to lady, obviously enquiring after her riding skills and preferences, and then calling forward a groom with a suitable horse in each case. Charity very much suspected that the mares and geldings presented, already bearing sidesaddles, were the oldest and quietest horses which the estate could provide. It was the only way that she could see that he could ensure the safety of all concerned – because she was equally sure that Lady Anne and the like would lie about their degree of competence, to avoid appearing in any way diminished.

They were all fools if they did, for as soon as the horses moved out of the stable yard, that competence, or lack thereof, would be instantly discernable.

Beneath her, Sage sidled, eager to be off, and Charity gentled her, knowing that she might not get a chance to truly let the mare run this day. The Duke finally had the last of the ladies allocated a horse, and the grooms led them to queue at the mounting block – Charity was so very glad that she could mount by herself! She watched as he went to Valiant, swinging into the saddle with an easy grace.

He turned the stallion, and rode to the side of the yard nearest the lane. She urged Sage forward, and joined him there. Once she was very close, he spoke softly.

"I expect this to be a truly terrible experience, Lady Charity. Please do take care, for I would not be surprised if one of them attempted to obstruct your path at some point. Or perhaps that might happen accidentally..."

"Is that, Your Grace, a reflection of your assessment of their... experience...?"

He laughed quietly.

"Yes, Lady Charity, you could express it that way."

They were then joined by the other gentlemen, and they lapsed into companionable silence, watching as the grooms finally got the ladies onto their horses. Once they were mounted, they all looked at least mildly capable, which Charity found a relief – if any of them had been completely useless, then the entire ride would have been, by necessity, at a walk.

They set off down the lane, the Duke providing commentary on the lands around them. The winter sun was pleasant, if not particularly warm, and the ground underfoot rather muddy and slippery in places, where the sun had melted the previous day's light snow. Sage was surefooted, and Charity gave herself over to enjoying the ride, despite the chattering flock of young women who surrounded her.

Ignoring them became remarkably challenging, however, when Lady Anne rode up alongside her.

"You match so well, Lady Charity... your hair, your habit, and your horse's coat – one might almost think that you had planned it that way..."

Not I, but the Duchess...

The thought slipped into her mind, but she did not voice it. Instead, she smiled faintly and shrugged.

"Simply a lucky circumstance, Lady Anne."

The woman tilted her chin up, and sniffed, as if she did not believe a word of it. Charity said nothing, and simply rode on, surreptitiously watching the manner in which the other ladies rode. None of them showed any sign of great skill, nor of any sensitivity towards their mounts.

They reached the gate in the lane, and the Duke opened it.

Charity rode through, reflecting on just how different it was from their ride that early morning. Sage stepped forward eagerly, a spring in her step, obviously hoping to be allowed to gallop across the fields again. Charity held her back, waiting to see what would happen. Once everyone was through the gate, the Duke spoke up.

"Shall we essay a canter across the fields, ladies and gentlemen?"

Lady Anne immediately agreed, but Charity thought that Miss Woodfield looked rather unsure. Still, they all nodded, and the Duke turned, and sent Valiant forward without a further word. Charity allowed Sage to move into a smooth, ground eating canter – but one which was nowhere near as fast as a gallop might have been. She glanced back to see Miss Woodfield clutch at her horse's mane, looking rather unstable as the stolid gelding launched into a rolling gait, following the other horses. The others fared only a little better, and Charity was hard put not to laugh.

Then, as she turned to look forward again, a thunder of hooves approached her on her right. Even as her mind was recognising the sound, and wondering who it was moving at such a pace, another horse slammed into Sage's shoulder. The mare staggered, then gathered herself, leaping forward. Charity stayed with her, trusting her to rebalance herself. As she did, the other horse charged past her, and Charity saw that it was Lady Anne, her face white, clutching desperately at the horse's mane and the saddle pommel, trying to keep her balance. Whatever had happened – and Charity suspected that it had been done on purpose - it had not achieved Lady Anne's aim – for now, her horse was out of control, bolting towards the cliffs. As Charity watched, one of the Duke's gentlemen friends went after her.

Charity urged Sage forward until she came up beside the Duke, who met her eyes, then raised an eyebrow.

"For whatever purpose, she rode right into me. But Sage is sensible, and surefooted. I do believe that Lady Anne overestimated her own abilities, and rather than her actions making me look bad, she seems to have quite clearly illustrated her own skill level."

"I see. I will make sure that Sage is thoroughly checked when we return – and you – you are not harmed in any way?"

"I am not. A little shaken, for it took me by surprise – but it takes far more than that to unseat me."

"Good, I thought as much – but I would not wish you to be harmed."

There was something in the way that he said it which made her feel suddenly heated. She looked away, towards the cliffs, where the gentleman had come level with Lady Anne's horse, and was even now bringing it back to a sedate pace, leaning across to hold its bridle and force it to slow.

When they all reached that point, they paused for some time – to look at the view, the Duke said, but Charity knew that he meant to give them time to recover their equanimity. The other young ladies clustered around Lady Anne, twittering away at her – from what Charity could tell, they were proclaiming how brave she had been. She shook her head, disgusted, and simply sat beside the Duke, and looked out over the sea.

Chapter Ten

Rafe watched Lady Charity from under lowered lashes as she stared out over the waves. She seemed so composed, and he admired her – for that steadiness, when she had just been effectively attacked, as well as for her superlative riding, which had seen her stay in the saddle and keep well in control throughout. Which was far more than could be said for Lady Anne.

Now, more than ever, he could see how much better a person Lady Charity was than all of the rest. But – what did she think of him? What did she truly want, in her life? He did not know, and the more he came to see that she was the only woman here he might contemplate choosing, the more worried he was that by doing so, he might be forcing her to something she did not want.

He still had some days until he must make that decision – days in which he might spend more time with her, if he could arrange it, and attempt to discover her thoughts. He reached out, without thought, and touched her arm gently. She turned those deep violet eyes to him.

Then she glanced down to where his hand still rested on her arm. He removed it. She frowned.

"Lady Charity, should we start back now, do you think?"

She looked around, taking in the others of their party, and then nodded.

"I think so. And at a very sedate pace, I believe. I am of the opinion that the ladies are more used to rides which are a walk up and down Rotten Row, for the sake of being seen, rather than a ride to actually move at any speed at all."

"That is most likely correct."

He turned away from her, and went to the others where they clustered, still, around Lady Anne.

"Ladies and gentlemen, it is time for us to start back to the house. We will go via the home farm lane – over this way, if you will follow me."

Miss Woodfield spoke, her voice hesitant and shaky.

"Might we... might we only proceed slowly, Your Grace?"

Rafe gave a half bow in the saddle.

"As you wish, Miss Woodfield. Please follow me. Petersham – I'll leave you to continue assisting Lady Anne, if you will?"

Lord Petersham nodded, and Rafe set off, pleased that he did not have to deal with the obnoxious Lady Anne himself. The ride back seemed interminable, and he made certain to stay near the other men, rather than any of the ladies, even though he would have preferred to ride with Lady Charity – he could not allow the others to think that he favoured her – even if he did.

That thought gave him pause. He did favour her – there was no longer any question of it. But did she favour him, at all?

*****

The remainder of that day, after the rather eventful riding party, Charity avoided everyone. She sat through dinner quietly, only speaking to her mother, and then claimed that her megrim had returned, and went to her room. The Duke met her eyes as she turned to leave, concern etched on his features for just a moment. It made her heart thunder, but she steadfastly chided herself not to hope. He was simply concerned for his guest – there was nothing more to it than that.

But when she went upstairs, she paused outside the door to her guest suite. Either side of the door, an arrangement of dried flowers stood in matching elegant vases. But something seemed different – and then she saw it – a feather, tucked in amongst the dried leaves. A feather in graduated shades of brown, like those found in pheasant's tails. She plucked it out with a smile, and went inside the room, feeling, just from that simple thing, immensely better.

The next morning, she had thought to rise early and walk again, but was greeted by the sound of steady rain. So she lay in bed for another luxurious hour, then called for breakfast in her room. Today, no matter what, she did not intend to allow Lady Anne to disrupt her life. Quite why Lady Anne and her friends felt the need to harass her, Charity did not know – for she could not imagine that they truly thought her competition for the Duke's attention. She was, however, beginning to think that the Duke was unlikely to choose a bride from amongst them. None of them seemed the sort of person whom he could be comfortable with, could find affection with, long term. She shook her head – that was not hers to worry about – what the Duke chose to do was his own private business.

After she had dressed and eaten, she took her basket, with her sewing materials and all of the feathers she had left neatly packed into it, and went down the servants' stairs, then slipped along the rear hallway to the conservatory. She hoped that no one would find her there, amongst the plants, and it was warm, and a pleasant place to work. Perhaps, by mid-afternoon, she might finish the brooch she was working on, and perhaps another hat piece.

The conservatory was empty, and to one side there was a small table and two chairs, placed so that the plants surrounded them, making it almost seem as if one was outdoors. Even with the steady rain running down the glass panes, the light was good, and the sense of the place peaceful.

She settled in to work, her materials laid out around her – the basket on the other chair, and the feathers lined up by colour and type across one side of the table, the pieces in progress in front of her. It was, perhaps, rash of her to work on them outside her rooms, but the location was more pleasant and the light better. Besides – she had seen no sign that the other women had ever gone much further in this house than the parlour and the dining room.

More than an hour passed – she had no true sense of the time, and there was no clock in the room – as she became completely absorbed in her work. Creating things which were beautiful was most satisfying, and distracted her from all of the demands of daily life – including the fact that her mother had asked her, again, this morning, if she thought that the Duke was developing an interest in her.

The feather which had been in the arrangement at her door was the perfect piece for the latest hat decoration, layered with stronger coloured feathers, and held in place by a string of tiny pearls.

The pearls she had reused from a broken necklace which she had found in her grandmother's old trinket box – they were too small for the fashions of today's necklaces, but perfect to accentuate the hat piece. They were also fiddly and tedious to sew on, and required her complete attention to get right.

"Lady Charity! Whatever are you doing?"

The voice broke her concentration, and she looked up, annoyed, and answered without pausing to think.

"What does it look like I am doing? I am constructing a decoration for a hat, from feathers and pearls."

There was a gasp, and Charity realised, far too late, what she had done. Lady Anne stood before her, her face a picture of horror.

"You... are you telling me that you make things to wear... like a milliner, or a seamstress? You... work...?

Charity swallowed. This was a nightmare come true. Lady Anne would not be able to resist sharing gossip like this – and the word would no doubt run through the house party in a flash – that Lady Charity Pemberton stooped so low as to do the work of a commoner. And with that, every previous whisper about their family's financial situation would resurface too.

But it was too late – Lady Anne had seen, and Charity had admitted it. All she could do was attempt to mitigate it, at least a little.

"I create things for my own pleasure. I would hardly call it work."

Lady Anne regarded her as she might a cockroach.

"Ladies do not make things for themselves, when there are milliners and the like to do it for them."

And with that, the woman simply turned on her heel and exited the room, leaving Charity sitting there, torn between near hysterical laughter and tears. Well, apart from anything else, this would guarantee that the Duke would never be interested in her – a woman who made things like this was definitely not the *ton's* opinion of Duchess material!

Slowly, she packed all of her things away into the basket. Now, the steady beat of the rain on the glass panes of the conservatory seemed most appropriate – like tears for all that she had lost, for her inability to be the woman she should be, again.

*****

"Have you made a decision yet?"

Rafe shook his head. He sat in his mother's private parlour, a tea tray between them, as the steady rain ran down the window pane.

"I have not. I can conclusively say that there are a number of them I will not consider. Starting with Lady Anne. But amongst the others, I have not reached a decision."

The Duchess sipped her tea, and frowned at him.

"There are only a very small number of days left to Christmas, Rafael. You must choose soon. For myself – I would have thought that the choice might have become obvious by now – but if you are not sure yet, then you must redouble your efforts to speak with them, to assess which one you think you could come to bear an affection for."

Even as he shook his head again, the image of Lady Charity came to his mind.

She was certainly more pleasant than any of the others – but would she welcome his suit? Did she wish to marry? Or was she here because her family required her to be? And, most important of all, could she come to feel any affection for him?

He would have to find some way to ask her – about her feelings on the matter, without declaring himself prematurely. Perhaps a quiet ride together on the morrow? He would attempt to invite her to that, tonight.

"I will mother – but I will not rush, I will not risk making the wrong choice, just by wanting this whole process over. I will tell you my decision, by Christmas Day, as I vowed."

The Duchess regarded him with an expression which he could almost have interpreted as amusement – but she said nothing more, simply sipping her tea.

*****

When Rafe entered the parlour before dinner, he found himself automatically looking for Lady Charity. She was seated beside her mother on a couch near the fire, wearing a gown which was stunning, although simple, in a vibrant violet colour which he was sure matched her eyes. It was a far darker colour than young women usually wore, but she carried it off well.

He scanned the rest of the room, and noted that all of the other young women were present – all gathered together to one side. In contrast to Lady Charity's vibrant gown, they were all dressed in varying pastel shades. Clustered together as they were, they rather reminded him of a pale cluster of hydrangea flowers, past their summer prime, and fading.

It was not, he acknowledged, a flattering comparison, but it was the image which had popped into his mind. They seemed to be whispering amongst themselves, and punctuating whatever was being said with little gasps and sideways glances – glances in Lady Charity's direction. He wondered, immediately, exactly what they were discussing – and whether it represented a new way in which they planned to torment Lady Charity.

Casually, he circulated in the room, speaking to various of the older people, and to his gentlemen friends, before moving carefully to place himself close to where the young women gossiped. Fortuitously, Lady Waterton, who was his great-aunt, and somewhat hard of hearing, was seated close to them. He dropped into the chair beside her, and she nodded, smiling, not expecting him to actually talk. He settled himself to eavesdrop.

"Surely not! You cannot mean it!"

That was Miss Woodfield, he thought.

"I am completely serious – I saw it with my own eyes – and she even admitted it, outright!"

And that was Lady Anne, unmistakeably.

"But... where was she, how did you come to discover this?"

Lady Anne's voice lowered, taking on the sort of tone which indicated that this was a shocking part of the tale.

"It was quite scandalous – after all, she was in a place where anyone might have come upon her, as I did."

"Shocking!"

By now Rafe was fascinated – Lady Anne was quite a storyteller, keeping her audience hanging upon her every word. He, as much as they, wanted to know what the scandal was.

"It was – I near fainted at the sight. She was in the conservatory – I had asked a maid if there was a conservatory, just from curiosity, for the rain had made the morning so dismal. The maid directed me there, and you can imagine my horror when I entered to find her there, sitting at a little table, with the evidence of her shame spread all over that table."

There were gasps again, and Rafe stifled laughter – Lady Anne belonged on the stage.

"What, exactly, was she doing, Lady Anne?"

"She was... making things... with feathers, and pearls, and sewing thread. Making the sort of things that a milliner might make, with her own hands."

"Making things?"

"Yes, making things – like a commoner. Doing work unsuited for a lady!"

"But... why would she do such a thing?"

"When I asked, she claimed that she did it for her own pleasure – can you imagine that? It's enough to make me feel quite ill. I knew that she had nothing in the way of social graces, but this! Really, I can't imagine that she will ever be accepted in society again once people hear about this!"

Rafe sat there, listening to them continue to witter on about how shocking it was, but his mind was whirling. Now, he knew what she did with the feathers – and he was, far from horrified, rather impressed. She did something useful with them, instead of just collecting them to display somewhere! More and more, he was coming to realise that Lady Charity was the only woman at this house party that he could ever consider marrying. It was time for him to get serious about discovering what she thought.

He rose, nodding to his great aunt, and resumed his circulating in the room, eventually coming to stand close beside where Lady Charity sat. She looked up, meeting his eyes, and hers were full of misery – she obviously knew that she was being gossiped about.

He had a momentary urge to pull her to her feet, and into his arms, to console her, and wipe that misery from her gaze. That impulse shocked him, and he held himself perfectly still for a moment, considering it. Then, after being sure that her mother was completely engaged in conversation, he spoke in a whisper.

"Lady Charity, might I suggest a ride, very early tomorrow?"

Despite that misery, for a moment, there was a smile, and the light of something positive in her eyes.

"Yes, that would be wonderful, Your Grace."

"Dawn, then."

He gave her a small bow, and as he did, he pulled a feather from the bundle which never left his person of late, and, as he turned away to seek his gentlemen friends, he allowed the feather to drop from his fingers, to land in her lap.

Chapter Eleven

The next morning was blessedly clear. Charity slipped out of the house as the pre-dawn light began to paint the eastern sky in shades of faded rose. Her thoughts were no less in turmoil than they had been the previous afternoon and evening. That turmoil was not just from the fraught question of what to do about the gossip which Lady Anne and the other young women would spread amongst the *ton* once this house party had concluded - but also from the question of what the Duke had meant by dropping that feather into her lap at that moment. For he had, almost certainly, heard the gossip – heard about the true extent of Charity's failings, with regard to possibly being a suitable choice for his Duchess.

That he had still asked her to ride with him this morning seemed very odd – unless it was simply an act of friendship – an attempt to make up to her, in some small way, for the fact that she was his guest, and was being treated badly – even if it was not in any way his fault. Perhaps she should not have agreed – but she could not bring herself to miss the chance to ride.

Sage greeted her with a soft whicker and a nudge of her nose, and Charity thought, with wry amusement, that at least horses did not judge a person by anything other than their basic character. The Duke appeared beside her as she led Sage into the stableyard, Valiant's reins looped over his arm.

"Good morning, Lady Charity. I thought that, today, we might go the other way along the coast, towards where the river meets the sea. It is quite pretty, with a number of streams coming down to join the river along the way. And it is far less visible from the house."

Charity winced internally at his words – that such a thing should need to be a consideration both annoyed her, and made her embarrassed – for it was her peace of mind that he hoped to protect from Lady Anne and the like. She met his eyes and smiled, determined not to let him see how much the last few days had discomposed her.

"That sounds delightful, Your Grace."

At that moment, Simms came out with the gelding he would ride, following them, and Charity mounted up, hoping that the feel of a horse beneath her, and the clean cold air, would restore her spirits.

The frosty ground crunched under the horses' hooves as they went down the lane, and Charity automatically scanned the hedges as they passed, hoping to find feathers caught amongst the leaves. When she saw one, she urged Sage up onto the narrow verge, and stretched for it, glad that the horse gave her extra height to reach it.

Only then did she consider that the Duke was likely watching her, and she felt her cheeks flush red. Now she had foolishly reminded him of the content of the gossip! What must he think of her?

She tucked the feather in between the buttons of her habit, and urged Sage on down the lane. The Duke moved Valiant closer beside her, and, after a moment of quiet, began to speak.

"Lady Charity... might I... might I be so familiar as to enquire about what happened yesterday morning, which resulted in Lady Anne being so... vocal... about her opinions?"

Charity's heart sank. She could not, politely, refuse to speak at all, yet she did not wish to discuss it, no matter how kindly he approached the matter. She would have to answer – honestly, but in a manner which would hopefully allow her to avoid any further discussion.

"Your Grace, it is of no import – it was my own fault, for choosing to go to the conservatory, rather than staying in my own rooms. Lady Anne happened upon me, and her reaction was far more negative than I might have hoped."

There. That was honest, without delving too deeply into the matter – hopefully, he would let the discussion end at this point. She did not meet his eyes, but instead kept hers turned to the lane ahead. They had passed the stile, and the gate, and were now approaching the final end of the lane, where another gate blocked it completely. He was silent beside her, with no sound but that of the horses' hooves on the earth beneath them, and hope rose in her that he might allow the subject to drop.

He opened the gate, and she rode through. The fields stretched before her, with a line of scattered trees in the middle distance indicating the likely location of one of the streams that he had mentioned. Sage sidled, keen to be off, feeling Charity's disquiet and agitation. The Duke's voice came again.

"Lady Charity, I cannot see that you should blame yourself for Lady Anne's propensity for turning anything she can to gossip."

Charity turned to him, and the words tumbled forth, before she could call them back.

"Perhaps not – but I can blame myself for doing something which provided her with material ideally suited to gossip about! I should have known better than to do as I did."

"But... if what I heard is true, I do not, entirely, see why she believes your actions to be so terrible. It is not as if you operate a milliner's shop!"

Charity swallowed, suddenly on the edge of tears.

If only he knew the truth of it, of just how close to that she was, with supplying ready made pieces to the milliner in the town near their estate, through the intermediary agency of Maggie... he would no doubt be as horrified as Lady Anne had been.

Yet the small amounts of money that those pieces had returned were what had allowed them to keep all of the servants on, over the last two years of poor crops, rather than having to turn some of them off. She could not regret what she had done, and when she had told Lady Anne that she made the pieces for the pleasure of it, that had also been true.

She did not know what to do, and the urge to escape the moment overwhelmed her.

"You do not know... I..."

She shook her head, and gave in to the need to flee. She turned Sage, and sent her forward into a gallop, towards those trees which indicated a stream. The mare stretched out beneath her, happy to run, knowing that her rider wanted to escape something, and willingly attempting to help her do so. The fields flew past, the grass uneven beneath the mare, winter sere and thin, small bushes scattered about.

Perhaps the pace was unwise, on ground that she had not seen before, but, in the moment, she did not care. The line of trees was rapidly approaching, but, she discovered, there was another stream between her and them – a dip in the land had hidden it, and now, as she crested the slight rise, she was upon it. She would have to jump – the water was too close, at the speed they were going, for her to do anything else.

Sage saw it, and felt Charity's hesitation, for the water was wider than she had thought at first sight – a very big jump to ask of the mare, with no idea what unevenness hid beneath that water, if they did not clear it cleanly. The mare went towards it, until, at the last moment, she attempted to stop, slid, and then, realising that she was too close, launched into the jump regardless.

Charity rocked and teetered on the saddle, her knee clenched tight around the pommel, fighting to keep her seat, to give the mare enough free rein for her to achieve the jump. It was the closest she had come to falling in a very long time. But she did not fall. Sage landed, right on the far edge of the water, skidded slightly on the muddy ground, then managed to lift herself back into the gallop.

Charity sank back into place, and concentrated on bringing the mare back down through canter, to a trot, and then a steady walk.

She had been a fool, again. In front of the Duke, again.

Now, he would most likely remonstrate with her about that foolishness – and he would be right to do so for, by her actions, she had endangered Sage, as well as herself.

*****

Rafe struggled to understand what he had done, why his words had caused Lady Charity to flee him, as she had. Did she believe herself to be as beyond the pale as Lady Anne had declared her? That would be madness – yet... there she was, riding ahead of him as if demons chased her.

After the initial moment of shock, when Rafe had simply watched, startled, he had urged the stallion to follow, and Valiant had leapt forward, as glad to run as the mare. Now, he was gaining on Lady Charity but, he realised as she did not slow, she did not know the lay of the land. Fear filled him – fear for her – for he knew every inch of his estates and she was approaching, at a madcap pace, a wide stream which lay concealed by the rolling land.

He pushed Valiant on harder, knowing, even as he did so, that he could not reach her, or slow her, in time. He crested that small rise to see Sage jib at the edge of the water, then launch herself into the jump, desperately reaching for it, with Lady Charity teetering on the saddle, barely holding balance. Even as cold terror filled him, in the depths of his mind he admired her anew – somehow, even as she fought to keep herself in the saddle, she managed not to haul on the mare's mouth, not to disturb Sage's courageous effort to clear the stream, but to help her instead.

He had never before seen a woman ride so well.

His heart pounded, and, as Valiant gathered himself to make that same jump, Rafe's focus was all on the woman ahead of him. Valiant landed, neatly, and Rafe could see that Lady Charity had settled back into her normal stable position on the mare, and was even now bringing her back to a slower pace. But the sight did not remove the ice of fear from his heart – instead, it drove him into a moment of utter clarity.

He had nearly lost her.

She could have fallen, could have landed on the rocks which the bitterly cold water hid, and been badly hurt, even killed. If not for her superlative skill on a horse, he might have lost her – and that was a possibility he could not bear the thought of.

He had come to care for her. Perhaps even more than simply care... She was nothing like any of the other young women of the *ton* – she did not, in most ways, fit any of the things that society deemed 'required' for a woman who would be a Duchess – and yet, the very things which society judged her for were the things that he valued about her, that he admired about her.

He wanted, when the arrival of Christmas forced him to make a choice, to choose her – he knew that, now, with complete certainty. What he did not know, was how she would react when he declared himself to her. Any of the other young women would accept gushingly, and lord it over the others, revelling in having been chosen to be his wife. But Lady Charity... he was not sure what she would do – might she reject him? It was a thought that left him feeling terrified again – for, if she did, he would have to turn to one of the others – one of the women he did not like, let alone love.

Love.

The word rang in his thoughts like a bell, even as he reached her, and pulled Valiant back to a walk beside her. He swallowed, hard. He loved her. Somehow, one quiet walk, ride, or baldly honest conversation at a time, she had become the centre of his being. But how could he tell her that, and have her believe him, given that everyone knew this house party to be, rather than just about Christmas, a bride-choosing event?

He would work it out – he had to.

"Lady Charity – are you well? You did not suffer any injury during that rather dramatic leap?"

She turned to meet his eyes, her expression truly startled, and a sheen of unshed tears made their deep violet depths glitter. He waited, unsure – her expression was odd – as if she had expected him to utter very different words.

"I... Your Grace... Thank you for your concern. I apologise for endangering Sage by my foolish actions."

Rafe gaped at her, shocked yet again at how unselfish she was in her approach to life.

"My Lady, there is no need to apologise – you could not have known that the stream was there, given the lay of the land. And... I believe that I am the one who should apologise – for it was my words which sent you off at such speed – I did not intend to upset you so."

A single tear escaped, leaving a trail down her cheek.

"I am a fool, Your Grace. I know that making things, as I do, is something which most of the *ton* regard as utterly beyond the pale. They would not mind if I just collected the feathers, and displayed them somewhere, but the fact that I make them into something useful... that horrifies them. But I have learnt, since the terrible crops we have had in the last two years, that there is no dignity in being poor. I will admit to you my greatest sin – at least in the eyes of the *ton* – I do work – many of those brooches and hat pieces I make with the feathers that I find are then sold, in the milliner's shop in the town nearest our estate. The milliner does not know that I am the one who makes them, but they are still sold. Without that money, we would have had to put off staff this year."

Rafe was, now, genuinely shocked – but not because what she had done was wrong – far from it – he found her even more admirable now. She had found a way to use the skills and resources she had, to improve a difficult situation, to take care of the staff of their estates, when otherwise those people would have suffered hardship. No one should be mocked or decried for taking care of those in their employ. He was shocked because he had never before met a woman of the *ton* who was so practical, and so selfless. That she should be treated like a pariah as a result was unconscionable!

"Lady Charity..."

"I know. I should not have done it, and I should certainly not have been such a goose as to allow myself to work on the pieces anywhere where someone else might come upon me. But now that Lady Anne knows, even part of it, there will be gossip, which will spread through the *ton*, and my reputation will be ruined as a result. I will understand if you should wish me to leave – I would not want my foolishness to tarnish anyone else's reputation."

Rafe could not bear it – he reached out and folded his hand over hers where she held the reins lightly. Startled eyes met his. He tightened his fingers on her hand.

"Lady Charity, I do not despise you for what you do – rather, I admire you. You have turned something useless into something useful, you have chosen to assist those less fortunate than you, and you have comported yourself with dignity and kindness, no matter how others have behaved towards you. I do not see any part of this which warrants anything other than admiration."

She turned her head away, but not before he had seen another tear trail down her cheek.

Gently, he used the hand which held hers to encourage her to bring Sage to a halt, even as he stopped Valiant. They came to stillness beside each other, her head still turned away.

He dropped his reins on Valiant's neck, and reached to cup her cheek, turning her face back towards him. Tear drenched violet eyes met his. Drawn by an irresistible magnetism, he leaned across, and brought his lips to hers, even as his thumb gently brushed the tears from her face.

She gave a little gasp, and he deepened the kiss, tracing her lips with his tongue. She did not pull away – in fact, after a moment of stillness, she moved her lips on his – a soft exploration which sent his heart racing.

Perhaps, what he now most desperately wished was possible, after all.

Chapter Twelve

He was kissing her. She had just admitted her disgrace to him, and instead of turning away, he was kissing her.

Charity was most glad of the solid form of the horse beneath her, for without it, she suspected that she would have fallen, her knees having gone unaccountably weak at the sensation of the Duke's lips on hers. In that moment, as she tentatively returned his kiss, she realised how badly she had been deceiving herself these last few days. She had come to care for him, deeply, and had been determinedly telling herself that it was not so. Now, with his lips on hers, it was no longer something which she could deny.

Did this... did this mean that he cared for her too? She did not know – the moment was confusing, and wonderful, all at once. Eventually, he drew back, and she met his eyes, uncertain. His gaze held only warmth, and she felt an echoing heat fill her body.

She did not know what to do, or say.

After a moment of silence, the Duke smiled.

"Lady Charity, convention has it that I should not have done that, that I should apologise profusely for so accosting you – but... I cannot regret it, and in the light of our agreement to speak honestly to each other... I believe that I have wished to do that for some time now, but I have not been, at all, sure of how you felt about me."

"I... do not object, Your Grace. But... what you said... about admiring me for what I did. How can that be? The things that I have done are completely against what is expected of a Lady of quality."

"I have, over this past year, come to believe that what is expected of a Lady of quality has nothing to do with what I, personally, value in a woman. And if those expectations produce women like Lady Anne, then I find them sadly lacking."

"Oh... I... I don't quite know what to say, except perhaps that I wish more gentlemen thought that way."

He smiled again, that smile which lit his face and made her heart beat even faster than it already was.

"Shall we ride on? I do believe that Simms has just reached the point where he can see us again..."

Charity blushed – when the Duke had kissed her, she had not, for one moment, thought of the groom who followed them... if he had seen such a thing... If he had, would he have told anyone? She did not know – and if he had, what would she have done? For such a situation would have called for the Duke to marry her – it was what they had come here, hoping for – but... if he was to marry her, she would have it be because he had made that choice himself, hopefully as a result of feeling something for her, not because of a compromise.

She was not like Lady Anne!

And he had said that he believed a marriage should be between people who actually at least liked each other...

They rode on, and in one way, it felt as if that kiss had never happened – in another, everything had changed. That companionable feel which had been between them now felt somewhat more strained, with the spectre of the kiss, and what remained unsaid, hanging over them.

Would he ask her to be his bride? Or was this just a moment where he had allowed friendship and concern for her distress to give the impression of more? The rest of the ride passed quietly, and they spoke of inconsequential things, both caught up in their own thoughts.

Back at the stables, she spent a moment with Sage, then, thanking the Duke, slipped inside and up to her rooms, hoping that, this time, no one would see her.

*****

Rafe watched her walk away, going back to the house, back into the endless round of polite society conversation, and the hopes and expectations of Lady Anne and the like. He wanted to call her back, to kiss her again, to ask her... Was he really ready to take that step?

He was not sure – the whole incident had left him shaken, and still very uncertain of her feelings – feelings which had come to be more important to him than his own. That uncertainty stayed with him, a deep-seated discomfort, throughout the morning.

By early afternoon, when he went into the parlour, unable to avoid it any longer, he felt irritable and most unsociable – but also compelled to be there, to talk to them all, not just because of his vow to his mother, but because he wanted to be there, should Lady Charity need defending from the machinations of Lady Anne.

As always, of late, he tucked the bundle of feathers into his waistcoat – perhaps he might have a chance to leave one for her. It was a strange whimsy, that he kept collecting them, kept leaving them – after the one he had dropped directly into her lap, she undoubtedly now knew that it was he who left them for her – yet she had not mentioned it – was that, he wondered, because of her terrible embarrassment and shame about making things with them?

He stepped into the parlour, and automatically scanned the room. She wasn't there. The disappointment was acute.

He went to where his mother sat, even though she was in conversation with Lady Chilwinth – for at least being with his mother made it a little harder for the young women to brazenly crowd him. The Duchess looked up as he approached, her expression a silent question. He shook his head slightly, and simply settled into a nearby chair and accepted a cup of tea from the maid. It was not long before Lady Anne found reason to come to her mother, and then, because he was close, of course she spoke to him.

"Good day, Your Grace. The weather today is far better, don't you think? If we are lucky, Christmas Day will be clear and bright."

He forced himself not to grimace. He hated social chatter about nothing. She fluttered her eyelashes at him, and gave him that false sweet smile.

In his mind's eye, he saw Lady Charity, as she had been out on the cliffs, that first morning they had ridden together, her smile wide and genuinely happy, her rich red hair a little disordered from the breeze. They had spoken of bluntness and honesty. The contrast to the woman before him was sharp, and further drove the resolve within him.

Today, tomorrow at the latest, he must speak to Lady Charity, and tell her of his feelings, and ask her...

He had a vow to fulfil, and the deadline was fast approaching. But, in most ways, that no longer mattered – what mattered was that he loved Lady Charity, that she was everything he wanted, and nothing that he had expected, nor that society suggested she should be. He did not care one whit about society – but did she?

He pulled his thoughts back to the moment, and favoured Lady Anne with a stern glare – she recoiled a little.

"I am sure that we will all have a pleasant Christmas Day, regardless of what the weather is like, Lady Anne."

At that moment, the Duchess took note of the conversation, and rescued him.

"Lady Anne, I have activities planned which will be possible, regardless of how the weather turns out. I am quite certain that we will all enjoy ourselves."

"Of course, Your Grace."

Rafe finished the last of his tea, and stood.

"If you will excuse me, I must speak to some of my other guests."

He rose, bowed, and left her there, going first to his gentlemen friends.

Lord Petersham raised an eyebrow as Rafe stopped beside him.

"Lady Anne seems determined to draw your attention, but could it be that you are intentionally avoiding her?"

"Very astute of you, Petersham. I find the Lady rather... overblown for my tastes."

"Overblown? I appreciate a woman with some opulence to her – especially one who seems as willing to please as Lady Anne."

"If that is how you think, feel free to pursue her – she is on my 'absolutely not' list. In fact, if you feel inclined to distract her over the next few days, I will be eternally grateful."

"So – if she is off the list, does that mean that all of the others are still potentials? Or have you come to a decision...?"

Rafe looked at him and laughed.

"Even if I have, there is no possible way that I will tell you, or anyone else, until the Lady in question has accepted my offer."

Petersham shrugged.

"A man has to ask."

"Indeed. But for now, that's the only answer you'll get. Shall we escape this, and have a game of billiards, once I have circulated a little? I find the company in this room rather stifling this afternoon."

"Billiards sounds like a capital idea, Oakmoor. I'll slip along there now and set the table up."

Rafe nodded, and turned away from Petersham, steeling himself to deal with the other young women. Where was Lady Charity? Her absence worried him, greatly.

*****

The day was passing, and Charity knew that she should go downstairs. Her mother would worry, if she did not do so soon. But she could not. Not now.

In her hand, she held the note – she had read it over and over, but the words stayed the same – words she could not escape. Words which would steal the hope from her, the hope which had only just burst into being, due to a kiss out on the fields this morning. The note had been slipped under her door, mid-morning, as she had sat working on the next feathered hat piece for her mother.

There was no signature – but she did not need one to know who had sent it. It could only have come from Lady Anne. The words were stark on the page.

> *'If you wish to retain your reputation, and that of your family, then you will not put yourself in the Duke's path. If you attempt to engage his affections, I will ensure that all society knows of your disgrace, in a suitably dramatic manner, which will make you, and your parents, social outcasts. Do be sensible, and do not aspire to a station above that which you deserve.'*

She could not do that to her mother! Could not, after all of her mother's work to scrimp and save enough for Charity to have decent gowns and a chance at a good match, throw all of that away, and leave her mother outcast from society.

Which meant that, somehow, she had to avoid the Duke, even though all she wanted was to be with him, to be kissed by him.

She would have to stay in her rooms, and, if her mother came to see why, she would claim a megrim again, and take to her bed, if necessary, to convince her mother that it was true. That might work for the rest of today, but what would she do on the morrow?

For the first time in three years, she had no enthusiasm for creating. The feathers lay on the small desk in her room, silently accusing her – and reminding her of every moment when the Duke had left one for her, when he had aided and abetted her crimes, rather than mocking her. She wanted to cry. She had, finally, met a man who did not frighten her, who might understand her, who might allow her to do things that she liked, rather than expecting her to force herself to be someone she was not – and now, just when it seemed that she was lucky enough that he liked her, she would lose him. But it was a sacrifice she would make, for her family.

The afternoon wore on, and eventually, Charity rang for her maid, and asked Maggie to inform Lady Warkworth that she had a megrim. Maggie eyed her miserable face for a moment, then simply nodded, and went to deliver the message. But, when she came back, she had questions for her mistress, as Charity had known she would. The maid slipped back into the room, and locked the door behind her.

"I gather, my Lady, that you want to avoid everyone today? What has happened? For when you returned from your ride this morning, you looked quite happy. Can I help?"

Charity pushed the feathers aside – there was no possible way that she would do any good work today – not when every moment of it was a reminder of how badly she had erred. Maggie raised an eyebrow, then walked across the room, and gently packed it all away in Charity's basket.

"Thank you, Maggie."

"Lady Charity – is your distress to do with what happened with Lady Anne, yesterday? For all of the servants are talking about it – Lady Anne's maid is as much of a gossip as she is."

Charity felt positively ill at Maggie's words. She had known that Lady Anne would spread the gossip, painting Charity in the worst possible light, but she had not, until now, considered the fact that the servants would spread it too. She was, truly, doomed already – whether Lady Anne carried out the threat embodied in the note, or not, if the servants were already discussing it, it would seep out into the *ton*, regardless. Nothing could save her, or her mother, now.

Maggie waited, and Charity knew that she really should give her an answer. After a moment, she pulled the note from her pocket, and smoothed it out on the desk.

"This happened. It was slipped under the door a few hours ago."

Maggie stepped forward, and lifted the note. She frowned as she read it, puzzling out the words – for Maggie had only learnt to read in the last few years, with Charity's help. Her face paled as she read. Then she looked up and met Charity's eyes.

"That's terrible, Lady Charity! Who do you think sent it?"

"I cannot think that it was anyone other than Lady Anne. She… she has tried, at least once, to trap the Duke in a compromise – she appears quite thoroughly determined to be chosen as his bride. I cannot understand her thinking – for what man would choose a woman who has already tried to trap him?"

"I do not understand that either. And, from what I have seen, whether you went near him or not, I do not think that the Duke would ever choose her."

“I agree. But still, I cannot risk her doing something terrible, out of spite – what happens to me would only be the result of my own foolishness in taking my work down to the conservatory – but for her to harm my mother’s reputation as a result is unforgiveable – I cannot allow it to happen! But… if the servants are already gossiping, I do not know how I might prevent it.”

Maggie regarded her seriously, obviously thinking.

“My Lady… the only thing that I can think of, which would prevent the gossip from doing dreadful harm, would be if you married the Duke. For, if you did, his influence would far outweigh that of Lady Anne’s family… and there would be no point in her doing something dreadful to you, to keep you away from him, if he had already chosen you, and married you.”

Chapter Thirteen

Lady Charity had not come down at all that afternoon, nor had she been at dinner. Rafe worried, wondering why, especially as Lady Anne seemed remarkably cheerful, and thrust herself in his direction at every slightest opportunity, despite Petersham's attempts to distract her. By the end of the evening, he was glad to escape to his rooms, but Lady Charity's absence still worried him – after her upset that morning, he was concerned that, somehow, he had made it worse by that kiss – that she might be avoiding him.

It would break his heart if she was.

His valet had assisted him with changing into loose comfortable clothing, then Rafe had sent the man off to bed. He intended to simply sit and read, with a brandy, and let himself actually relax. Hosting a house party, where every young woman present was hoping to become your bride was a most exhausting and stressful business. But he could not concentrate on the book – the feeling of Lady Charity's lips beneath his kept replaying itself in his mind.

He had hoped to speak to her this evening, to find some quiet moment, to ascertain her feelings on the matter, and to admit his own. Now, worry filled him – worry which he had no remedy for. Then, as the house sank into the silence of night around him, there came a tap at his door. Curious, he rose, and went to open it, rather than simply bid whoever it was enter.

"Please, allow me in."

Startled, he stepped back, and two cloaked women entered the room. He shut the door, and turned the lock, quite sure that privacy was of the utmost importance – for he knew the voice which had spoken.

Lady Charity pushed her hood back, and met his eyes, hers full of a strange mixture of fear and defiance.

"This is my maid, Maggie." She gestured to the other woman, who dipped a curtsey. "She will wait in your dressing room if she may, to allow us privacy whilst still providing at least the veneer of propriety."

He nodded, completely puzzled, and a little alarmed by this late-night visit, but he waved to the door on the other side of the room.

"You will find it there. My valet has his own rooms, upstairs, so you will discover it to be unoccupied."

The maid turned, without a word, and went into his dressing room. He returned his gaze to Lady Charity.

"My Lady..."

"Please, Your Grace, let me speak, before I lose my courage entirely. I know that this must seem utterly outrageous of me, to appear in your rooms in the dead of night."

"As you wish, my Lady."

"I am about to be beyond forward, and ask you some questions which I pray you will be as honest in answering as you have ever been with me. I will not tell you the reason that I ask these questions, until after I hear your answers. Rest assured, I have very good reason for asking."

"I promise you my honesty, as I did that day on the cliffs."

Rafe found himself beyond curious, and completely puzzled. He was almost certain, now, that his fears of earlier were unfounded – these were not the actions of a woman who wished to avoid him. But still, he did not understand her purpose in being here – if she did not despise him, after that kiss, could it be that she cared for him? Was there cause for hope?

"Thank you. My first question is – is it true that you have committed to choosing a bride by Christmas Day?"

"It is – a year ago, I vowed to my mother that I would choose a woman to marry, by this coming Christmas Day. I am a man of my word – although I will admit that I did not expect it to be as difficult a challenge as it has been."

She inclined her head, her deep violet eyes examining him, as if they might learn some deep truth from his appearance.

"It had seemed rather arbitrary to me, but that explains it. Now, leaving that matter aside for a moment, my next question. Have you... or could you... come to care for me, at least a little?"

Rafe studied her face – she was absolutely in earnest, it appeared. He could, at that point, have burst into laughter – for there he had been agonising about how he might get a chance to admit his feelings to her, and here she was, demanding that admission. He swallowed the urge – laughter would create entirely the wrong impression.

"Lady Charity, before I answer you, let me say that I have spent today considering how I might get the chance to be alone with you, so that I might tell you of my feelings. The fact that you have appeared here, now, asking this question, has rather simplified that issue. Thank you. I wanted you to know, before I say this, that it is what I had hoped to say to you, had planned to say to you – this is not a statement born of this moment, but one I have come to, slowly, over the days since your arrival here. To put it baldly, yet with the greatest feeling I have within me – I love you Lady Charity."

She gasped, and wavered on her feet, yet a smile crept onto her face.

"I… Your Grace… I am beyond glad to hear you say that! For I have come to love you, too. But… I must ask you one further question, coming back to where I started, so to speak. As love is often not a consideration in society marriages, and as it has been rather dramatically proven that I have a large number of flaws in the eyes of society, I must know this. Is love enough for you to choose me as your bride, or will you choose another who is better suited, in society's eyes, for the role of your Duchess?"

Her voice shook a little as she spoke those last words, but she stood firm before him, her eyes never leaving his. He took the three steps which brought him to stand before her.

"I told you, that first day, that I hoped to marry someone I at least liked, preferably loved – I meant it. Nothing outweighs love."

"Then, before you say any more, I will tell you why I took the extreme measure of coming here, tonight. I spoke the truth, when I said that I love you – never doubt it – but I am here, now, because other circumstances made it critical that we knew each other's minds on this matter, as soon as possible."

"That sounds rather mysterious, and dramatic."

"It does, doesn't it? It is, in a way. This afternoon, I received a note – it was slipped under the door to my rooms. The note bore no signature, but the likely author was not hard to imagine. It threatened me, and my family, with the utter ruination of our reputations. And the price for which the writer would be so kind as to not carry out that threat – was for me to go nowhere near you."

Rafe gasped, shocked.

"That is unforgiveable! And you suspect...?"

"I am almost certain that the author of the note is Lady Anne. I am not willing to allow my own foolishness to destroy my mother's reputation in society, as well as my own – but I was faced with the question – what could I do to prevent it?"

"And, obviously, you came to an answer to that question?"

"I did. My thoughts were as follows – even if I stayed away from you, she might still, just out of spite, choose to spread the gossip – indeed, it is already circulating amongst the servants, so stopping it is unlikely at this point. Therefore, complying with the demand was pointless. But... I still needed a solution which would stop the gossip, or at least mean that it did as little damage as possible. And the only one that Maggie, or I, could imagine would work, was if you married me. Then, gossip could not change what you did, and Lady Anne could no longer hope that you would choose her. In addition, your influence is far greater than her family's, and that would, to a large extent, protect my family, as they would be, by marriage, associated with you. So... I came to ask, to discover if marrying me was something which you could, in any way, countenance – for though I love you, I would not wish you to marry me, if you did not feel that you might at least come to care for me."

Rafe could wait no longer – he took her hands, and pulled her into his arms, bringing his lips down on hers as she gasped in surprise. This time, he kissed her without reservation, all of the desire which had been growing within him expressed in that moment. She melted against him, returning the kiss.

When, eventually, they drew apart, they were both flushed, and breathing hard.

"Lady Charity – I would have you know that, even before I realised that I had come to love you, I had concluded that, of all of the women here, you were the only one whom I could countenance marrying."

"But… all of the ways in which I am unsuitable…."

"Are all of the things that I love about you. Society's opinion is irrelevant – if we are to live with each other for the rest of our lives, then what we want, and like, is far more important."

"Your Grace… did you… do you mean…"

"Yes – marry me, Lady Charity Pemberton, and let us be defiantly happy together."

She clung to him for a moment, her eyes glistening with unshed tears, then rose on her toes and brought her lips to his.

"Yes."

The word was a soft exhalation, before their lips met in another deep kiss.

*****

When the kiss ended, Charity stepped back, feeling weak-kneed.

This was better than she had dared to imagine – that he loved her was the stuff of dreams, and she felt positively giddy. He smiled at her, a smile full of promise for the future, then he turned, and she wondered where he was going. She watched as he went to a small escritoire, and opened its drawer to take something out. He came back to her, and held out his hand.

"Charity... if I may be so bold as to call you so... I make you a gift – something between us, with meaning only for us. I have collected these, from that very first morning when I saw you in the lane – it just seemed the right thing to do. And then, when I had no way to gift them to you directly, I began leaving them in places where I hoped that you would find them. Since that day, a bundle of feathers has been on my person at all times. Now, I gift you these – the remaining part of that bundle, and I ask that you make something with them – something to wear for our wedding."

Charity felt as if her heart might explode with happiness. It was, without doubt, the best gift that she had ever been given. She took them from his hand, their colours glowing even in the dim light of the candle lit room, and smiled.

"Thank you. And – thank you for caring – every feather you left for me made a difference to how I felt, on that day. I will be delighted to make something beautiful from these. But... what happens next? Will you... will you announce our betrothal on the morrow?"

"I will. And I will take great delight, unchristian of me though that is, in watching Lady Anne's face as I do so. I will, of course, warn my mother first, and I ask that you warn yours – I gather that there will be no objection from your family, to this match?"

"Mother and Father will be delighted – indeed, Mother hoped for this outcome, even though I doubted."

"Then your mother is a wise woman. As is mine – I suspect that she realised I loved you, even before I did. Come, much though I would hold you in my arms forever, you must return to your rooms – you will need sleep to face the day ahead."

His words filled her with warmth – she would be very happy to be held in his arms all night!

"Indeed, I will." She went to the door of the dressing room, and tapped. "Maggie, you can come out now."

The door opened, and Maggie came out. She paused, studying Charity's face for a moment, then turned to the Duke.

"Forgive me for my impudence, Your Grace, but may I ask – might it be the case that I can be the first to congratulate you?"

He laughed – a sound of joy, and genuine amusement.

"You may, Maggie – and yes, congratulations are in order. You must make your mistress look beautiful tomorrow – and fill her with confidence – she is a far better person than those who sought to harm her." Charity blushed at his words of praise. He came to her, and bent to press a kiss to her cheek. "Good night, Charity."

"Good night... oh! I don't know your forename, Your Grace."

"Rafael – but please, call me Rafe."

"Good night, Rafe."

With that, he opened the door and cautiously looked out, as Charity waited. He waved them forward and Charity and Maggie pulled the hoods up over their heads. The hallway was completely empty as they slipped through the shadows, back to Charity's room.

Sleep came to her surprisingly fast, and was filled with dreams of Rafe, of kisses, and more.

*****

"Mother, I have good news for you."

"I see – so, you've finally come to your senses, and realised the truth of what was right in front of you all the time, have you?"

"Ah... I..."

"You are about to tell me that you've chosen Lady Charity, aren't you? And that she has accepted?"

Chagrin filled Rafe – he had been right, his mother had known all along.

"Yes, and Yes. I intend to make an announcement now, in the parlour, once everyone has gathered. Do watch Lady Anne closely – she attempted something deeply unforgiveable yesterday, something well beyond just the gossip, and if Lady Charity was not as courageous as she is, things might have ended very differently."

"Oh? Well, you can tell me the details later. Let us go to the parlour, and get this announcement done. This year has been wearing for both of us – but I am pleased that you have kept your vow – you have always been a man of your word, as was your father."

*****

Charity had not thought it possible to be more afraid than she had been, as she stepped into Rafe's rooms last night – but, apparently, it was.

Now, as she sat in the parlour, under Lady Anne's venomous glare, terror filled her. What if she had dreamed it all? What if Rafe did not make the announcement she expected?

She forced herself to sip her tea, and listen to what Miss Penelope Woodfield was saying to the older ladies – something about the activities which the Duchess had arranged for tomorrow. For Christmas. Tomorrow was Christmas Day, today was Christmas Eve. Somehow, the time had passed to bring them to this moment, all whilst she was distracted by falling in love with the Duke... Rafe...

The parlour was full, with everyone except Rafe and his mother present, almost as if they all expected an announcement. Perhaps they did, for, after all, every rumour had said that he was to pick a bride by Christmas Day. The door clicked open. Every head in the room, including hers, turned in that direction.

Rafe walked in, and went to stand near the fireplace, not far from where Charity sat. His mother quietly settled into her favourite chair. The room was silent, and Charity watched as Rafe looked around, making sure that everyone was present. That done, he gave a small nod, and smiled.

"Ladies and gentlemen, I believe that you are all expecting an announcement from me. It has been a poorly kept secret indeed that I have intended, from the start, to choose a bride before Christmas Day."

A whisper ran around the room, and all of the young women looked at each other with annoyed expressions, as if believing that one of their number had been chosen, and had kept that information from the others. Charity stifled a laugh. Lady Anne looked positively thunderous, and Miss Woodfield mournful. Rafe was toying with them, repaying them, a little, for the manner in which they had hounded him.

Silence fell again, and he continued.

"I have made my choice. I have asked the lady in question to marry me, and she has accepted my offer. I hereby announce my betrothal."

Lady Anne emitted a gasp, then clenched her jaw, her eyes finally finding Charity, filled with disbelief and anger. The Duke turned towards Charity and held out his hand. She rose, gathering every ounce of her courage about her, and went to stand beside him. He entwined his fingers with hers, and spoke again.

"Lady Charity Pemberton has done me the honour of agreeing to become my wife."

There were seconds of utter silence, then a scatter of applause. Applause which almost, but not quite, covered the fact that Lady Anne uttered a stifled sob as she left the room. Then people came to them, offering congratulations, and Charity allowed all thought of Lady Anne to slip from her mind, so that she could concentrate on maintaining the dignity required of a Duchess to be.

*****

That evening, what had already been planned as a Ball, where people from neighbouring estates would attend as well, became a betrothal Ball. The Yule log was lit in the large fireplace of the main parlour, and the walls opened up between the three parlours to make one ballroom, large enough for this relatively small gathering. The Christmas decorations of holly, pine and ribbons made it beautiful.

But, truthfully, Charity would not have cared if she had been standing in a bare cold room, so long as Rafe was by her side.

Lady Anne and Lady Chilwinth had quietly departed Oakmoor Chase within the hour after the announcement – which Charity thought rather rude of them. Still, she was glad that they were gone, for now, nothing dimmed her happiness.

Epilogue

They had risen before dawn, and met each other in the stables, riding out to gallop across the fields to the cliffs. There, they had sat ahorse, close beside each other, with their hands entwined, and watched the sun rise over the sea. Gulls wheeled above them, and, as they finally turned to go back, a feather floated down from the sky, so close to them that Rafe reached out and caught it, passing it to Charity.

"Even the birds approve." She laughed, delighted. He looked at her, then raised her hand to his lips, turned it over and pressed a kiss to her palm. "I know that we will speak our formal vows in the church soon, but here, now, I choose to make a vow to you. I will always be honest with you, no matter what comes, for it was our ability to trust each other's honesty which saved us in the face of Lady Anne's threats and deception. I love you, Charity Pemberton."

"I return that vow – I will always be honest with you, no matter what comes. I love you, Rafe Livingstone."

They set off again, back to Oakmoor Chase, hands still entwined as they rode – for that morning, they were to be married, in the centuries old church in Oakmoor village.

*****

Rafe stood in the church, where he had so often listened to sermons, and yet, somehow, it seemed different, new, more beautiful. Ribbons and winter roses decorated everything, and the stained glass rose window cast a perfect rainbow rondel of light on the floor immediately inside the door.

Charity stepped into that pool of coloured light, and Rafe ceased to breathe. She was stunningly beautiful, her deep red hair glowing, and the tiny gems twisted into it sparking fire from the light. Her gown was a deep burgundy, the same colour as that riding habit, and absolutely perfect, with a glittering trail of gems in a design which looked like a cascade of falling feathers all down one side of it. Some of those feathers were real, pinned to the gown by the gems, others were only the illusion of feathers, in gold and silver thread, and sparkling gems.

It was, he thought, the best possible way in which she might have used the feathers he had given her – and the best possible statement of defiance of the *ton's* judgement which he could ever conceive of. A susurrus of whispers ran through the church as people realised what they were seeing – but it sounded, to him at least, to be composed of admiration, more than negativity.

She moved towards him, and he met her eyes. All else faded away.

When she reached him, they turned to the vicar, who smiled, and began. The vicar had known Rafe since he was born, and was overjoyed to marry him now. Perhaps, soon, there would be another small boy for him to baptise...

Soon, it was done, the words all spoken, and they were married, under God's sight. They stepped out into the late January morning, and saw the sun drawing glittering sparks from the still frosty ground, and the small icicles which remained on the more shaded parts of buildings and trees. The world was sparklingly perfect, just for them.

He led Charity to the carriage which would take them back to Oakmoor Chase, where the main ballroom had been opened up and decorated for the Wedding Breakfast. Once they were settled in the carriage, and it moved off, he pulled her into his arms, and kissed her.

After some time, they stopped kissing, she leant on his shoulder, and her voice came to him, whisper quiet.

"I never, ever imagined that I would be here, that you would see anything of value in me. No other gentleman ever did. And most women adjudged me awkward and socially inept, as well as plain. Yet you... you see me differently. Thank you."

"I never imagined this, either – I had almost resigned myself to a loveless marriage, just to ensure the continuance of the title. But I did not know what I was looking for, what it was about all of those other young women that made them unsuitable for me. Until I saw you – all of those things that you thought were wrong with you – those are the things which make you perfect for me. Thank you for being exactly as you are."

He kissed her again, and they did not cease kissing until the carriage rolled to a stop outside Oakmoor Chase.

The footman opened the door, and let down the steps. Rafe stepped out, then turned back as Charity went to exit – he scooped her into his arms before she put foot to step, and carried her, laughing, into the house.

The End.

I hope that you enjoyed
'The Duke's Christmas Vow'

You'll find a preview of another of my books, 'A Spinster for a Spy' just after the 'About the Author' section of this book.

About the Author

Arietta Richmond has been a compulsive reader and writer all her life. Whilst her reading has covered an enormous range of topics, history has always fascinated her, and historical novels have been amongst her favourite reading.

She has written a wide range of work, from business articles and other non-fiction works (published under a pen name) but fiction has always been a major part of her life. Now, her Regency Historical Romance books are finally being released. The Derbyshire Set is comprised of 11 novels (9 released so far). The 'His Majesty's Hounds' series is comprised of 17 novels, with the last now released.

She also has a number of standalone novels released, and four other series of novels in development. She lives in Australia, and when not reading or writing, likes to travel, and to see in person the places where history happened.

Be the first to know about it when Arietta's next book is released! Sign up to Arietta's newsletter at

http://www.ariettarichmond.com

When you do, you will receive two free subscriber exclusive books - **'A Gift of Love',** which is a prequel to the Derbyshire Set series, and ends on the day that 'The Earl's Unexpected Bride' begins, and **'Madame's Christmas Marquis'** which is an additional story in the His Majesty's Hounds series.

These stories are not for sale anywhere – they are absolutely exclusive to newsletter subscribers!

Connect with Arietta:

Follow her on Amazon - https://www.amazon.com/Arietta-Richmond/e/B016GG1KJ6/

Like her Facebook Page - https://www.facebook.com/AriettaRichmondAuthor

Follow her on Twitter - https://twitter.com/AriettaRichmond

Follow her on Instagram - https://www.instagram.com/AriettaRichmond/

Follow her on Bookbub – https://www.bookbub.com/authors/arietta-richmond

Follow her on Goodreads - https://www.goodreads.com/author/show/14508806.Arietta Richmond

Here is your preview of

A Spinster for a Spy

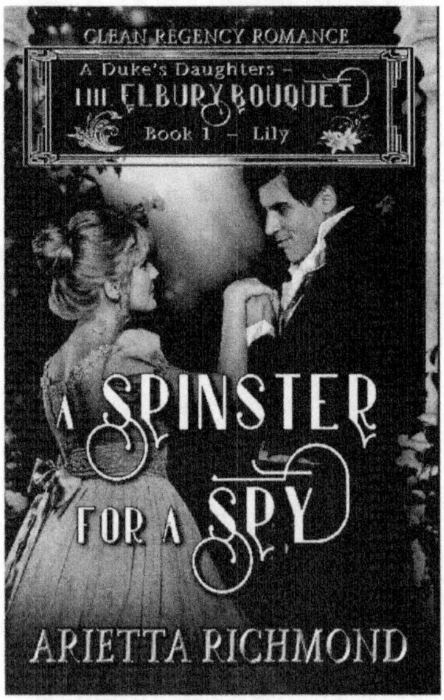

A Duke's Daughters –
The Elbury Bouquet - Book 1

Clean Regency Romance

Arietta Richmond

Chapter One

"You, my dear sister, are a spinster. You cannot deny it any longer."

Thorne Gardenbrook, Marquess of Wildenhall, smiled smugly at his sister as he spoke.

"I am not a spinster! Certainly, I may be older than the age at which most girls marry... but I simply have not yet found a man that I care to marry."

Lady Lily Gardenbrook glared at her brother. He shook his head sadly.

"You delude yourself, Lily. You are two and twenty, and this will be your fourth Season – why do you not choose a man – it's not as if you have no suitors. I have introduced you to half the *ton*, in this last few years!"

"I do not choose any of them, because they are all horrible! They care nothing for me, for who I am – all they see is a Duke's daughter with a large dowry, and a figure which is not unappealing."

Thorne laughed, but his expression was serious when he spoke next.

"You may well be right, but I do not know that you can hope for the sort of love that our parents have – and you have been hoping for that, haven't you? Very few are lucky enough to marry someone that they love. And, in the end, better a marriage based on simple liking, than a lifetime alone and lonely."

"I have, indeed, been hoping for love. I am not sure that I could live with someone I barely liked – and most of the eligible men I don't like at all. If you are so sure that I should find someone this Season, then you had best introduce me to some new possibilities – for I refuse to contemplate those I already know."

Thorne frowned, and Lily knew that he truly did care what happened to her, and to all of her sisters. As brothers went, he was good – generally helpful, protective, and even willing to join in with mischief at times. And, though she would not admit it to him, he was right – she needed to act soon, to find a man to marry – for her sisters were not married either, and she suspected that they were holding back until Lily married. She sighed, and forced a smile onto her face. Thorne frowned again, shaking his head.

"I will try – but, truthfully, those you have not met are not of the kind of character that I would have my sister marry. Rakes, gamblers and fortune hunters make up a deplorable amount of society."

"Thank you - trying is all that either of us can do."

Thorne rose, and left the room.

Lily leant back into the embrace of the old armchair, staring blankly into the flickering flames in the grate before her.

The book of poetry which she had been reading when Thorne came into the room still lay on her lap. Her fingers traced its cover, and her thoughts twisted in the never-ending circle that they had followed for three years now.

For there was more to her refusal of all suitors than simply the fact that none had inspired her to love. Her refusal was grounded in fear – a fear that her closely guarded secret would be discovered, that a husband would take from her the one thing which she most enjoyed. The thing which was, most certainly, not something which a lady of the *ton* could do, with the approval of society.

<<<< O >>>>

Trent Weatherton, Marquess of Canterford, inhaled deeply as he stepped through the door of Bigglesworth's Books. There was something about the scent of books which spoke to his soul, which brought to mind winter afternoons ensconced in his library, by the fire, with a volume of poetry, or perhaps a history, or even, though he would not admit it to other gentlemen, a novel.

Mr Bigglesworth greeted him with a smile.

"Good day to ye, my Lord. I've a few volumes I think you'll like, if you've the time after your meeting?"

"Excellent, Bigglesworth – I always have the time for books."

Bigglesworth waved him past, and he slipped through the dusty curtain behind the counter, and into the dimness of the back corridor.

The rickety looking stairs were silent beneath his feet, as always, and the ancient looking door at the top was solid beneath his fingers. He knocked.

"Enter."

The room was everything that might not be expected. It was large, clean, and well lit by large glass windows all along one side. A rug of a quality which would not be out of place in a stately home graced the floor, and the couches that surrounded it were exquisitely carved and upholstered. The man who rose from one of them to greet him was of middling height, unremarkable except for his piercing grey eyes.

Trent went forward to him.

"Lord Setford. I trust that your summons does not come due to bad news?"

"No, no. Nothing difficult this time, m'boy. Although you may not be enthusiastic about it. Do sit – the coffee is on the side table, if you've a mind to taste it."

"Your coffee is always worth drinking Lord Setford."

Trent sank onto the couch, and poured himself a cup of the strong bitter liquid from the pot that sat there. He marvelled, again, at how Setford always managed to have perfect coffee waiting, no matter when a man arrived at his door.

"Good, Good. Now, let's to business. You understand the scope of the responsibilities you've been granted, I trust?"

"I do, if that is no more or less than you previously told me."

"It is. But what you may not have truly grasped, is the way in which you might best achieve what is needed."

"Oh?"

"Yes – if you thought that what I asked would allow you to avoid society events – as I know you've had a tendency to do for this last year and more, since your father's death – then you were mistaken. That's what I wanted to discuss today. If you are going to serve the Crown by managing and preventing civil unrest and treasonous activities within England, then you will need to be always gathering intelligence – not simply through the men I have assigned you, but yourself. For the greatest threats to England have as often come from amongst our own, as from abroad, and from amongst the aristocracy in particular. The poor rarely have the money or the time to stir up trouble, unlike our peers."

Trent studied Setford's face, wondering where this was going.

"I can see the truth in that. But... what do you want me to do? I freely admit that I am still learning the techniques which you so effortlessly apply."

Setford laughed, a full rich sound, and nodded.

"And that is exactly why I chose you, Canterford. You are willing to learn – you are astute, and observant – and that is exactly what I am asking you to act on. I need you to get about in society more, to become the man who is invited to all of the major hostesses' events, who is so well known that no one looks at him twice. For when you achieve that, you can move among them, observing everything, and no one will notice you doing so. If you get it right, half of them will even tell you their secrets voluntarily."

Trent sat for a moment, staring out of the windows at the rooftops of London, where dirtied snow slowly melted on soot covered slate. He took a deep breath and turned back to Setford.

"You, my Lord, are quite the most devious man I have ever met."

Setford laughed again, and gave a little seated bow.

"Glad you've realised that, m'boy."

"You know full well that if you had spoken of this requirement, when we first discussed me joining the ranks of the King's spies, I would likely have refused you. Instead you played upon my sense of duty, and my need to do something more than manage my estates, to move past my grief at my father's death. And now that I have fully committed to you, to serving the Crown in this way, you drop this upon me. I shudder at the very thought of endless evenings spent in the ballrooms and salons of London, eyed off, like a prime piece of horseflesh in the ring at Tattersall's, by all of those husband-hunting young women."

"Which is exactly why you are the right man for the job. You'll be focussed on what needs to be done, not on carousing and flirting." Trent winced, but nodded. Setford had the right of it, and he would not attempt to back away from the course he had committed to. Honour demanded that he be true to his word. "I will make it a little easier for you – I can guarantee you invitations from quite a few who also have some... relationship... to our work, to smooth your way into it. But it is up to you to appear as carefree as possible – like a man recently released from mourning who relishes the chance to go about in society."

"I can act the part, but I can't promise not to curse you in the privacy of my mind, if I find it all unutterably tedious!"

Setford laughed that hearty laugh again.

"I can't ask more than that m'boy – and who knows, you might even enjoy some of it."

Trent nodded, but his expression was dubious enough that it drew another laugh from Setford. Ruefully, he found himself laughing too.

"Did I really look that horrified by the idea?"

"You did, m'boy, you did."

"Well then, I will need to practise my dissembling, won't I? We can't have the hostesses of society realising just what I really think of their balls and soirees."

"You will indeed. And you can start tomorrow."

Setford lifted an embossed card from the table beside him, and passed it to Trent. Trent took it, hesitantly, as if it might bite, somehow. He felt, in that instant, as if something portentous would be started, simply by the act of reading that card. He shook the whimsical thought aside, and bent his eyes to the card.

'The Duke and Duchess of Elbury would be pleased to welcome the Marquess of Canterford to a Soiree to be held at Elbury House.'

The direction followed, and the stated date of the event was, as Setford had said, the following day.

"What did you tell them of me?"

Setford smiled.

"Very little – except that you are a friend, recently out of mourning, and wishing to re-establish himself in society. But Marcus, the Duke, no matter how genially blustering he may appear, is as astute as you are – he will understand that I have a purpose in assisting you with invitations, and he will also know not to ask. Just attend, observe, and try to enjoy yourself and look natural."

Trent could not prevent the snort of laughter that escaped him.

"Look natural? I have never, in my life, truly been comfortable amongst crowds of my peers – so perhaps natural is the wrong word. But I will try to look as if I actually want to be there."

Continued…

I hope that you enjoyed this preview – read the rest at:

https://ariettarichmond.com/go/get-a-spinster-for-a-spy

Books in the A Duke's Daughters – the Elbury Bouquet Series

A Maiden for a Marquess (Iris) (coming soon)
A Heart for an Heir (Thorne) (coming soon)

Books in the His Majesty's Hounds Series

Claiming the Heart of a Duke

Intriguing the Viscount

Giving a Heart of Lace

Being Lady Harriet's Hero

Enchanting the Duke

Redeeming the Marquess

Finding the Duke's Heir

Winning the Merchant Earl

Healing Lord Barton

Kissing the Duke of Hearts

Loving the Bitter Baron

Falling for the Earl

Rescuing the Countess

Betting on a Lady's Heart

Attracting the Spymaster

Courting a Spinster for Christmas

Restoring the Earl's Honour

From Soldier Spy to Lord (Books 1 to 3 as a set)

To Love a Determined Lady (Books 4 to 6 as a set)

Love Heals a Lord (Books 7 to 9 as a set)

To Love a Dashing Lord (Books 10 to 13 as a set)

Books in The Derbyshire Set

The Earl's Unexpected Bride

The Captain's Compromised Heiress

The Viscount's Unsuitable Affair

The Count's Impetuous Seduction

The Rake's Unlikely Redemption

The Marquess' Scandalous Mistress

The Marchioness' Second Chance

A Viscount's Reluctant Passion

Lady Theodora's Christmas Wish

The Derbyshire Set Omnibus Edition Vol. 1 (the first three books all in one)

The Derbyshire Set Omnibus Edition Vol. 2 (the second three books all in one)

Regency Collections with Other Authors

Christmas Ever After

A Regency Romance Springtime Collection
Love, One Regency Spring

A Regency Romance Summer Collection
Love a Lord in Summer

A Regency Romance Summer Anthology
Regency Summer Escape

A Regency Romance Autumn Collection
Love in Autumn

Regency Christmas Proposal

A Regency Romance Christmas Collection
Love, One Regency Christmas

A Regency Romance Springtime Collection
Love, One Spring Season

A Regency Romance Summer Collection
Regency Summer

A Regency Romance Summer Anthology
Regency Summer Secrets and Soirees

A Regency Romance Christmas Anthology
A Regency Christmas Together

A Regency Romance Christmas Collection
Regency Christmas Delight

Books in the Regency Scandals Series

Books in the Nettlefold Chronicles

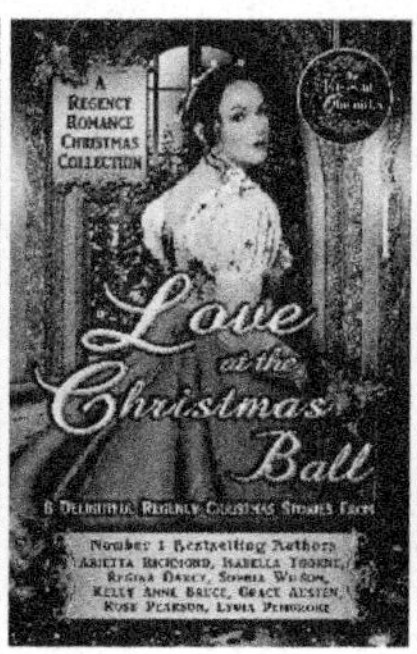

Other Books from Arietta

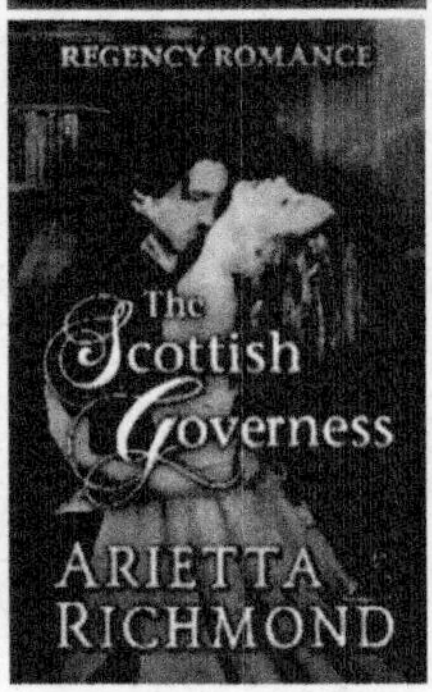

Themed Regency Collections

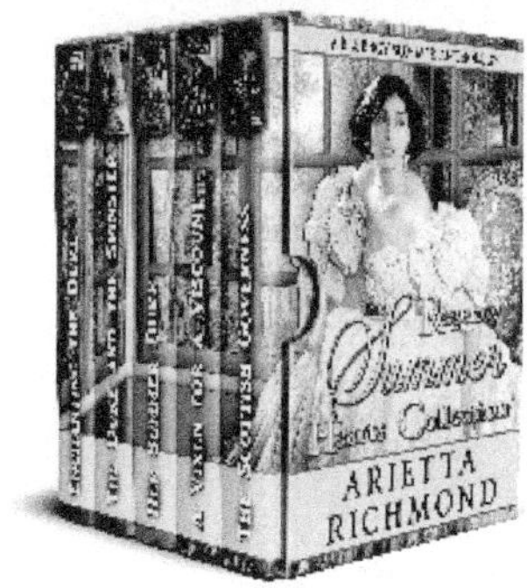

Other Books from Dreamstone Publishing

Dreamstone publishes books in a wide variety of categories ranging from Clean Romance to Erotica, to Kids Books, Books on Writing, Business Books, Photography, Cook Books, Diaries, Coloring books and much more. New books are released each month.

Be the first to know when our next books are coming out

Be first to get all the news – sign up for our newsletter at

http://www.dreamstonepublishing.com

Printed in Great Britain
by Amazon

36384211R00099